Were they ever goin[g] same room together wi[thout striking sparks] off each other?

Maybe Lola just needed to let go, give in and let fate take control.

"What exactly do you think is the right thing, Erik? Because I don't know anymore. What I do know is that being this close to you and not having the right to touch you makes me ache."

He closed his eyes briefly, then opened them. The heat that engulfed her left her skin feeling too tight to hold her in. "You always have the right to touch me, Lo. Any time. Any way."

Reaching out, Lola pressed her hand against the hard planes of his chest. The heat of his skin burned straight through her. Cool droplets clung to him, sparkling in the sunlight. And she was done denying what she wanted.

Leaning forward, Lola ran her tongue across his skin, collecting the droplets and savoring the taste of him.

"Lola," he groaned deep in his throat. The rumble of her name rolling off his tongue pulled any last resistance out from under her.

This was what she wanted. Erik was what she wanted.

And she was strong enough to take what was in front of her.

She'd worry about the aftermath later...

Dear Reader,

I'm so lucky to count several firefighters among my personal friends. They're the most honorable, dedicated and brave men and women I've ever met. As you can imagine, it was easy to envision a hero that possessed these same qualities. A man no one—including my heroine—could help but fall for...twice.

Erik McKnight definitely fits that bill, risking his own life over and over to save others. So what if he's got a reckless streak and a guilty conscience no sacrifice can seem to assuage? That is, until he returns home and finally confronts the chain of events that cost him everything—including the only woman he's ever loved.

In the course of writing *Up in Flames* I had the honor of accompanying several local firefighters on a ride-along. The guys were more than willing to share all the aspects of their job, giving me an amazing glimpse into the reality of their lives. We won't talk about how the jacket absolutely swallowed me whole! Or how inadequate I felt watching them move like a well-oiled machine to help someone with a serious medical issue. But we can talk about how that experience solidified for me just how much we all owe these men and women who sacrifice time from their families in order to protect others.

I've been privileged over the past few years to support a charity that provides financial support to local firefighters who are sick or injured. If you'd like to donate, please feel free to visit www.imathlete.com/donate/brothersforlifebenefitfund.

I hope you enjoy reading Erik and Lola's story! I'd love to hear from you at kirasinclair.com, or come chat with me on Twitter, @KiraSinclair.

Best wishes,

Kira

Kira Sinclair

Up in Flames

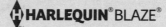

Recycling programs
for this product may
not exist in your area.

ISBN-13: 978-0-373-79965-7

Up in Flames

Printed in U.S.A.

Kira Sinclair writes emotional, passionate contemporary romances. A double winner of the National Readers' Choice Award, her first foray into writing fiction was for a high school English assignment. Nothing could dampen her enthusiasm... not even being forced to read the love story aloud to the class. Writing about sexy heroes and strong women has always excited her. She lives with her two beautiful daughters in North Alabama. Kira loves to hear from readers at kirasinclair.com.

Books by Kira Sinclair

Harlequin Blaze

The Risk-Taker
She's No Angel
The Devil She Knows
Captivate Me
Testing the Limits
Bring Me to Life
Handle Me
Rescue Me

SEALs of Fortune

Under the Surface
In Too Deep
Under Pressure

To get the inside scoop on Harlequin Blaze and its talented writers, visit Facebook.com/BlazeAuthors.

All backlist available in ebook format.

Visit the Author Profile page at Harlequin.com for more titles.

I'd like to dedicate *Up In Flames* to all the men and women who serve the Decatur, Alabama, fire and rescue department, especially Brandon Strickland. Thank you all for your service and sacrifice.

1

"LOOKING GOOD, as always, babe," Sean said. Lola Whittaker frowned as he slung his arm around her waist, pulling her into the warmth of his body even as his fingers dipped dangerously close to her butt.

It was a familiar gesture, one that said he was comfortable touching her. Lola wished she felt the same. With a shake of her head, she dropped one hand from the camera she'd been holding up to her eye and used the easy excuse to direct his hand higher. "I'm working."

What was wrong with her? Sean Morris was a good guy. Easygoing, intelligent, honorable. Sexy as hell in a boy next door kinda way. He'd asked her out several times over the past few months, and while her head said she should give him a chance…she'd never found a reason to say yes.

Considering he worked as a firefighter for her dad, she had two good reasons to say no.

Lola twisted her fingers into her worn camera strap. The camera *he'd* given her so many years ago. The

one she couldn't get rid of, no matter that she'd up-
graded to a newer model at the studio. Whenever she
took photographs just for herself, this was the camera
she pulled out.

A good reminder why getting involved with Sean—
or any firefighter—was a bad idea. She'd already
messed with one and had the battle scars to prove it.
She wasn't ready to jump into something with another
guy who embraced danger for a living, even for a noble
cause.

"Get your hand away from my sister's ass, you
moron," Colton drawled, punctuating his order with a
smack across Sean's arm.

Sean laughed good-naturedly, holding his hands up
and backing slowly away. "I'll just go sweet-talk a slice
of cake from Mrs. Monahan."

"You do that," Colt grumbled. Her brother steered
his wheelchair beside her, looking out over the group
of people scattered across the park. The Memorial
Day family picnic was a tradition, one her grandfather
started. He'd been fire chief in Sweetheart, South Carolina, before her own dad had taken over twelve years
ago.

Both of her sisters had come into town for the long
weekend. Over by the tables, her older sister, Suzi, bus-
tled to organize the casseroles, congealed salads and
fixings that appeared at every Southern potluck. Her
younger sister, Kayla, type A extraordinaire, was busy
grouping the desserts by type. Heaven forbid that pies,
cakes, brownies and cookies comingled.

Memories of her mom filling that role, organizing

things in her quiet, authoritative way, reared up. A stab of pain accompanied the memory. It had been fourteen years since they'd lost her to a drunk driver, but the pain never seemed to go away. Lola had simply gotten used to living with that hole in her heart.

Her father, along with half the Sweetheart fire brigade, stood around the exceedingly huge grill. She wouldn't have been surprised if several of them were grunting like cavemen as they stared at the obscene amount of sizzling meat.

Raising her camera again, Lola snapped a quick picture, somehow managing to capture the pride and contentment on her dad's face. There was nothing he loved better than having all of his team gathered around him.

Wives and girlfriends clustered together, chatting and intermittently hollering at kids as they tore through the town park.

This was home. Family.

Lola had worked hard to find her place in the sleepy little town she loved so much. She was proud of the successful business she owned. Between graduation pictures, spring family portraits and wedding season, she'd barely had a weekend off in months. She loved, absolutely loved, what she did and was so lucky to be able to make a living at it.

So why had she felt so restless lately?

It was hard to put her finger on it, but even now, during the weekend that she looked forward to every year, she couldn't shake her sense of disquiet. Not even the weight of a camera in her hand calmed her—and it had always calmed her before.

Frustrated with herself, Lola tried to refocus on the view through her lens. She walked several paces closer to the playground, crouching down to capture action shots of the Mitchell twins. At four, both boys were holy terrors, but adorable ones.

Spinning in place, Lola tracked across the gathered group, looking for other moments to capture.

"Sis, why don't you put the camera away and enjoy the party?"

She was so used to the quiet whoosh of Colton's tires across grass and gravel that she hadn't even heard him follow her. But she should have known he wouldn't be far behind.

He'd been her right hand for the past six years…ever since the accident. They'd always been close, two years apart, sandwiched between Suzi and Kayla, but working together had only strengthened the bond between them.

That and almost losing him.

"Try interacting with folks for a change instead of just watching through that camera of yours. Remember? I purposely left this weekend open so you could take a few days off. But in order for that to happen, you actually need to put down the camera."

Lola breathed deeply and tried not to let her bad mood spill out over her big brother. He was just trying to be helpful, although this conversation was becoming increasingly frequent—not to mention increasingly annoying.

"I enjoy having a camera in my hand, Colt. You know that."

"Sure, but every now and again you need to engage

with people. You know, create your own memories instead of preserving other people's."

With a sigh, Lola cradled the camera in her palm
and let it drop to her side. "Fine." If for no other reason
than to get him off her back, she walked to the parking
lot. Popping the hatch on her small SUV, she carefully
packed her camera back into the worn padded bag.

The sound of crunching gravel whispered behind her,
but Lola ignored it. No doubt a late arrival to the festivi-
ties. Stepping back, she slammed the door shut, whirled
around and barreled straight into a solid wall of muscle.

Her body reacted, shock and awareness crash-
ing through her. Heavy hands gripped her shoulders,
steadying her. Electricity crackled across her skin.

A lump formed in her throat. She recognized him
long before her gaze could travel up to take in his face.
But she knew. Her body remembered. Reacted.

All too much.

Slowly Lola's gaze tracked up from the center of a
wide chest, over unbelievably rounded shoulders, up
the long column of a thick throat to the eyes that still
haunted her dreams—and her nightmares.

Those familiar smoky grays stared back at her, som-
ber and searching. The impact of him was unexpected.
Heat erupted across her skin, radiating out from where
he held her like fire consuming paper. The few other
times she'd seen him over the years, she'd been prepared. Knew Erik was in town.

Today she wasn't ready. Her mouth was bone dry. So
many emotions careened through her. She had about as

much control as a runaway car in the middle of an action movie. Which pissed her off.

Correction—the man touching her like he still had the right to pissed her off.

Jerking away from him, Lola sucked in a harsh breath.

"Lola. It's good to see you."

"Erik. I can't say the same."

That wasn't strictly true. Because even as anger—anger she'd been harboring for the last six years—burst through her, she couldn't stop her gaze from ripping down his body. Cataloging the differences and ensuring herself he was whole and safe.

He was bigger—pure muscle. Considering the work he did now, that was no surprise. Smoke jumping wasn't for weaklings. It was, however, for daredevils and adrenaline junkies. Erik McKnight was both.

Hurt flashed through his eyes but was gone before she could even blink. Rocking back on his heels, he stuffed both hands into his jeans pockets. "I'm sorry you still feel that way."

Wow, so he'd finally issued her an apology. Hardly for the right reasons, though.

"What are you doing here?"

"Didn't your dad or Colt tell you?"

No, obviously they hadn't. But her anger now had a new direction, and the minute she was finished here they were both going to get a serious tongue lashing. The men in her life were all oblivious morons.

"I'm—" his gaze pulled away, focusing on the sky behind her "—taking a couple months off."

There was a story there. Six years ago she would

have asked for an explanation. Today she didn't want to care, so she kept her mouth shut.

The smile he flashed her was without any of the humor that usually lit his face. "Came home to spend some time with Mom. Your dad's letting me pick up some shifts at the station."

Oh, goody.

Lola nodded, because what else was she supposed to do? "Well, good luck with that." Hooking her thumb over her shoulder, she said, "I'm just gonna go…"

"…do anything that gets you far away from me."

"You said it, not me."

"That doesn't make it untrue."

She shrugged. He wasn't wrong, but her mother had raised her to be too polite to say so.

Putting one foot behind the other, she slowly backed away a short distance before he said, "You look good, Lola. I… I really am glad we ran into each other."

Was he serious? Lola stared at him for several seconds, searching his face before she realized that he was. Which made the anger bubbling up inside her finally burst free.

"Did you take a hit to the head, Erik? You act like I haven't been right here for the past six years, exactly where you left me when you ran away. Ran away when my brother was lying in a hospital bed, broken and bleeding."

"Because I put him there." Erik's gruff voice whispered over her, a swell of words that made her insides quake with the memories of those horrible days following Colt's accident.

"You're right. You did." The accusation she'd wanted to scream at him for so long fell between them like a whisper through a quiet church.

But she didn't feel any better. In fact, the ache in her chest felt worse.

"That, right there, is why I left. I could see it every time you looked at me."

"See what?"

"Blame." His stark expression ripped through her. And she'd be lying if she didn't acknowledge the small part of her that wanted to reach out to him and offer him comfort.

But he was right. She did blame him. For so many things.

A blast of childlike laughter startled her as a couple of kids darted through the corner of the parking lot several feet away.

No, she wasn't having this conversation here, now. It wasn't the time.

"Whatever." Lola started to take a step back again. "It's ancient history and no longer matters."

"Lo." Sean walked up next to her, startling her as he flung an arm around her waist again. This time, she didn't correct him when his fingers swept dangerously close to her ass.

Erik's gaze narrowed, taking in the familiarity and comfort of Sean's embrace. She couldn't help delighting in his reaction.

But mostly she just wanted this encounter to end.

"I saved you a steak, but I can't fend off the vultures forever."

"Great," she said, looking up into his open expression.

Sean flashed her a smile, understanding and concern running beneath the surface. He squeezed at her hip, reassurance she didn't need but appreciated. Why couldn't she want him?

Holding out his other hand, Sean waited for Erik to shake it. "Erik, good to see you back, man. Thanks for picking up that shift for me. I really appreciate it."

Without waiting for a response, Sean swung them around, leading her in the direction of the pavilion. "Thanks," she murmured.

"Anything you need, beautiful. I'm your guy."

God, why couldn't that be true? Even now, she could feel the tingle of energy crackling across her skin. The fine hairs on the back of her neck were standing on end. Not because Sean was touching her, but because she could *feel* Erik's gaze raking down her spine.

He'd always had that effect on her. On her body. Lola couldn't remember a time when she hadn't wanted him. From the moment she'd discovered that boys were beautiful instead of gross, Erik McKnight had been the source of all her fantasies.

And apparently, not even Erik stomping on her heart was enough to halt her bone-deep reaction.

Lola fought the urge to glance back over her shoulder. Nope, she was stronger than that.

Or she wanted to be, because her body was still in a riot, even from the brief physical contact of his hard chest and muscled thighs.

Damn him for making her ache in a way no one else ever had.

"HERE, I THINK you need this." A day after running into Erik, Hope Harper plunked a shot glass down onto the table in front of Lola, spilling the amber liquid.

She wasn't wrong. "I shouldn't."

"Seriously, Lola, every girl deserves the numbness of alcohol when the ex unexpectedly shows up," Tatum Huntley drawled. She'd know, considering not long ago her husband returned from the dead after three years.

Picking up the glass, Lola took a deep breath, slammed the drink back and came up sputtering.

"Holy shit. I thought that was rum or something. Why would you give me cinnamon whiskey?"

Lexi Newcomb plopped back into her seat across the table. "I thought you liked cinnamon."

Lola did, but not when she wasn't expecting that kind of burn.

Looking at the women surrounding her, she was grateful that the minute she'd called on her friends they'd dropped everything to come ply her with alcohol and provide sound advice.

She definitely needed both right now.

"So, you literally turned around and ran straight into him?"

Lola wiped her hands down her face, hoping to erase the memory with the gesture. It didn't work. But her body was starting to feel warm—even warmer than memories of Erik usually left her—and some of the tension she'd been fighting since yesterday was easing out of her muscles.

"Yeah. Sean rescued me, not that I needed rescuing."

"Of course not," Hope said, patting her hand.

"Sean, huh?" The speculative look that Tatum passed across the table didn't do much to settle Lola's nerves.

"Nope, don't go there."

Easing back in her chair, her friend crossed her arms over her chest and raised a single eyebrow. "Why not?"

"Because the last thing I need is to encourage Sean. He's been trying to get me into bed for months."

"And remind me, why have you resisted?" Tatum asked. "He's hot, has a reputation for knowing exactly what he's doing in the bedroom, and you haven't exactly been burning up the sheets lately."

"Or ever," Willow Warwick tacked on in her soft way. That didn't quite kill Lola's twinge of embarrassment and annoyance—at herself. Her friends weren't wrong.

"We're not suggesting you become the Sweetheart slut, honey," Lexi said. "But there's nothing wrong with having a little fun now and again. A girl has needs."

Yeah, right. That was easy for them to say. They all had amazing husbands who were perfectly capable of meeting every one of their needs. They didn't remember how difficult it was to be single.

Lola looked around the table at the women staring earnestly back at her. Lexi she'd known almost all her life—their dads had been friends forever. Tatum had moved to Sweetheart several years ago. Lola had known Hope and Willow before, but they'd never been real friends.

Not until she'd moved back after college and opened her studio on Main Street, right down from Lexi's, Willow's and Tatum's shops and the newspaper office where Hope worked. In the past few years, they'd become so close that it felt like these women had always been a part of her life.

They knew everything, which sometimes was a curse more than a blessing.

Tatum's eyebrows beetled, her gaze swept across the table and, making a quick decision, she signaled their waitress for another round.

"No," Lola protested when she appeared with their drinks.

But Tatum ignored her. "Trust me, you're gonna need this," she said, holding out the second shot to her. "Because I'm about to lay something on you."

Lola stared at the glass for a couple of seconds, looked up into Tatum's steady gaze and decided *what the hell*. She tossed it back, the fire of it flaming in her belly.

"When's the last time you got laid? No, don't answer that because I already know. It's been months. Probably closer to a year. You need sex. To take the edge off. Especially with Erik back in town."

Tatum aimed a pointed look at her. "Trust me when I say I understand how difficult it is to resist falling back into bed with someone you have history with."

God, that was the last thing she needed right now. Even the thought of sleeping with Erik again sent heat straight through her. The problem was, the reaction was immediately chased by an icy cold that burned almost as much as the whiskey.

"Sean's been dancing around you for months. And

here's the thing. He's safe. Everyone knows he doesn't do permanent."

"What are you suggesting?"

"I'm suggesting that you fuck his brains out and take the edge off so you're not a lit fuse on a firework ready to explode every time you run into Erik. You know Erik's going to be working at the fire station—you're bound to see him. You can't avoid him altogether."

She could sure try. And maybe it was the two shots of whiskey talking—on top of the two beers she'd had before her friends decided she needed the hard stuff— but the idea of jumping Sean didn't sound completely asinine.

In fact, it sounded…perfect. Damn, she needed to get laid. Ever since running into Erik yesterday, her body had been a riot of reactions and nerves. And God knew that option wasn't any option at all.

She was *not* sleeping with Erik again. Period.

It wasn't that she wasn't attracted to Sean. She was. Who wouldn't be? He was fit, funny and sexy as hell. She just wasn't interested in anything deep with a guy who ran into burning buildings for a living.

If she was honest and up front with him about what this was, and what it wasn't…

The fire that had rolled into her belly along with the shots started to spread a pleasant warmth through her body.

Slowly Lola said, "Sean's working tonight." A plan began to form in her head. Lola had always been a woman of action. Once she made up her mind, she rarely saw any reason to delay executing.

Tatum's eyebrows shot up and a wicked smile twisted her mouth.

Hope said, "You've had a couple drinks, Lola. Are you sure you want to do this now?"

She shook her head, the room moving a little. "Why not? I mean, I don't necessarily need the liquid courage, but it can't hurt. Especially for what I've got in mind."

Pushing her chair back, Lola barely heard the loud scrape of legs against the wooden floor. "One of you ladies mind dropping me at the station?"

"You're sure?" Willow asked, staring up at her.

Lola nodded. "I need to do this." She needed to exorcise thoughts of Erik from her head—and memories of him from her body. The girls were right. She needed to take the edge off before she did something really stupid. It was going to be a long few weeks if she didn't.

Hope drove her to the front of the station. She offered to walk inside with her, but Lola refused. The station had been her second home all her life. She was comfortable there. Comfortable with the guys.

Although, it was late, creeping towards midnight, so most likely everyone would be catching some sleep.

The heat of the day had faded, and the pleasant breeze actually made her a little chilly. Wrapping her arms around her waist, Lola hugged herself. She tipped her head backward, taking in the brilliant stars shining through the black canvas of sky.

The world spun. Oh, maybe tipping her head back wasn't such a good idea.

She slipped into the station, registering that the engine sat silent, doors open and waiting, behind the huge rolling glass door. All the lights were out, except the few they kept burning around the clock.

Lola tiptoed down the hall toward the honeycomb of rooms the guys used on shift. She'd been here a million times, even occasionally in the middle of the night, when she was younger and visiting her father. When she got older it was to see Colt or Erik.

Nope, she wasn't thinking about him tonight. This was about exorcising Erik from her body and mind, not taking a stroll down memory lane.

Each shift was made up of four positions, each with a separate room, several beds filling the space so that every guy had his own whenever he was on. They all had lockers for their belongings. Despite the close quarters, she knew from personal experience that the rooms were surprisingly soundproof.

Which was a good thing, considering what she planned.

Lola paused outside Sean's room. Butterflies twisted through her belly. Or maybe that was the whiskey.

Either way, now that she was here, she was determined to see this through.

Standing at the doorway, Lola began to strip, letting her clothes drop softly to the floor. She stopped at her bra and panties, her bravado only carrying her so far.

She could just see the outline of his long body beneath the thin sheet. Lola paused at the edge of the bed.

Should she wake him up now, or crawl in with him first?

Deciding she was in for a penny, in for a pound, Lola reached for the sheet. His back was to her, naked, moonlight streaming across all his rippling muscles and broad shoulders.

Dropping down onto the mattress, Lola snuggled up against him. She ran her fingers down the slope of his waist. Mmm, yummy. A buzz she'd never experienced with him before melted into her bloodstream. Maybe this was going to be better than she'd anticipated.

Pressing her mouth to the curve of his neck, she murmured, "I need you to touch me. Right now."

Beneath her hands, he stirred. His massive body shifted, rolled, and suddenly Lola found herself flat on her back, staring up into sleepy, half-lidded, gorgeous gray eyes.

Oh, shit. Sean did not have gray eyes.

2

Erik had no idea what the hell was going on. He'd been sound asleep one minute and had a warm, very willing woman pressed against him the next.

Used to going from zero to a thousand in the blink of an eye thanks to his job, Erik was absolutely, positively lucid as he rolled. Somewhere in the middle of the maneuver his brain kicked in and he knew the woman in his bed was Lola.

He recognized the feel of her. Her unique scent, something citrus with a spicy undertone. A brush of cinnamon now that had never been there before.

Even after six years, every detail about this woman was etched into his brain...right along with the ever present need for more of her.

So his body reacted, going stone hard in a split second. His burgeoning erection nestled between the soft heat of her thighs. Somehow he managed to bite back the groan climbing up his throat.

"What the hell?" he growled, his voice rough with sleep.

Even through the heavy darkness, Lola stared up at him with those rich brown eyes that had always had the ability to slam through him. Her face was so damn expressive.

And right now her expression was hazy and hot. She was as turned on as he was. Which wasn't helping. Her chest rose and fell on short breaths and her skin… God, touching her burned.

Involuntarily, his hips pulsed against her, rubbing his throbbing flesh into the cradle of her thighs. And Erik realized she was almost completely naked.

Miles of her silky, honey-toned skin spread out, just begging for him to taste her.

He wanted her. Needed her. Had missed her so much. But he was also wary and still reeling from the things she'd said yesterday. All true, but still…

Fingers tangled in her long, dark hair, Erik said, "A day ago you were condemning me, and now you're crawling into my bed half-naked? What gives, Lola?"

Her expression morphed, shuttered. Her gaze darted over his shoulder, focusing on something other than him. He didn't like that at all.

Lola shifted, this time not to get closer, but to slip away.

"Oh, no you don't." His fingers tightened, pulling her gaze back on his. "You're the one who climbed into my bed. I'm keeping you here until you explain what the hell is going on."

Tension tightened her body for several seconds before everything inside her just…relaxed, and she sank deeper into the mattress beneath the weight of his body.

"Nothing, Erik. Let me go."

He should. Deep down, Erik knew it. But the feel of her…having her in his bed again after all these years…

Softly his fingers untangled from her hair and trailed across the silky smooth skin of her cheek and jaw. Touching her was the most amazing form of torture. The kick of awareness and need would have brought him to his knees if he was upright.

This woman had always had the ability to cut straight through him. He'd wanted her since he was seventeen. It had taken him almost a year to convince her to go out with him. To look at him as something other than her big brother's best friend.

In those months he'd done everything he could to show her he was serious and not just looking for something quick and easy. And the day she'd finally agreed to go out with him…he'd never forget the powerful, joyful feeling that had swept through him. Or the delight and wonder in her expression when she'd opened the box to find the camera he'd saved six months to buy her. The extra hours he'd worked had been totally worth it.

He hadn't given her the gift just in the hopes of breaking through her defenses. He understood the reasons she'd resisted, but he'd always known they'd be amazing together.

At seventeen he'd been sure Lola Whittaker was the woman he wanted to spend the rest of his life with. And up until the day he'd almost killed her brother, that had continued to be the plan.

So, yes, he should listen and let her go.

But he couldn't. He might have left, but he'd never

let her go in his heart. Not really. Lola had haunted him for six years. He'd done the right thing once. Apparently he wasn't strong enough to do it again.

"I can't," he whispered right before his mouth claimed hers.

She stiffened, but the reaction lasted only a handful of seconds before she gripped his shoulders and pulled him closer. A sound leaked out of her throat, a cross between a groan and relief.

At a single swipe of his tongue across her lips, she parted her mouth and let him in. God, she tasted just like he remembered. Spearing his tongue deep inside her mouth, he stroked against her own silky tongue.

She sucked and nipped. Chased after him when he tried to pull away. "Easy, baby," he murmured. "I'm not going anywhere."

Her legs tangled with his, hands chasing urgently over hot skin. She was just as frantic for him, which settled something deep inside him.

Erik pulled back, needing to look at her. Take her in. *See* her again. His gaze scraped down her lush body, all golden skin and compact muscle. God, she was gorgeous. And he wasn't just talking about the outside.

Lola had always intrigued him. Even as a kid, her confidence and determination were enviable and contagious. She knew who she was and what she wanted. From the outside looking in, he didn't think she'd ever faltered or questioned her own path.

He was someone who always questioned who he was, where he was going and what his purpose was, so her attitude had been like a shining beacon, pulling him in.

Lola, eyes half-lidded and sparkling with promise, arched up. Reaching behind herself, she popped the clasp of her bra open. Shaking the straps down her arms, she tossed the thing to the floor.

Just as he'd remembered, even her breasts were that warm, golden tone. He wanted to run his tongue over every inch of her skin, breathe her in. Her dark, dusky nipples puckered hard, begging him to touch and taste.

She squirmed beneath his gaze, a flash of unease crossing her expression. "Don't," he whispered. Erik didn't think he could take it if she changed her mind. Not now.

"I don't do reckless," she murmured. And Erik knew just how true that statement was. Losing her mom so suddenly, living with her remaining parent risking his life every night…and then falling for Erik even after he started living the same life. That fear she'd kept bottled up had made her cautious, not that he blamed her.

Colt's accident had surely made her even more so.

His life, on the other hand, was nothing but reckless.

Erik shifted, ready to climb out of bed even though it was the last thing he really wanted.

But Lola's grip on him tightened, holding him in place. "Tonight I'm stepping outside my comfort zone," she whispered. "You walked away without giving me anything, Erik. Give me this."

Her words lanced through him, mixing pain into the pleasure that swamped his body. But he couldn't tell her no. Had never been able to tell her no. Which was why he'd texted that he was leaving—because he knew if he'd looked in her eyes and she'd asked him to stay, he would have.

The thought of watching the love she'd felt for him morph into accusation and loathing—blame he'd rightly deserved replacing everything they once shared—had nearly killed him.

Tomorrow they'd deal with whatever came next. Right now he just planned on loving her.

Her hips shifted beneath him, rubbing the moist heat of her sex over his throbbing erection. This time, Erik didn't bother trying to bite back the groan that twisted through him. Although he did smother it when he wrapped his lips around the irresistible flesh of her breast.

He sucked hard and then smoothed the flat of his tongue against the tight peak. Scraping his teeth softly up, he stopped, gently holding her nipple prisoner…and then blew. She writhed beneath him, her leg wrapping high on his hip.

"You were always so responsive," he growled, dragging his mouth, tongue and teeth over every inch he could reach.

"Only with you," she breathed.

A possessive sense of wonder slammed through him. His. Lola had always been his. But that possessiveness came with a dark edge, because while her statement made him feel powerful, it also made it glaringly obvious that he hadn't been the only man to touch her like this.

He had no right for that to piss him off. And yet it

did. She'd been a virgin when they'd come together. That had meant something to both of them.

Dammit, this was not the time or place for those thoughts.

Scooting down the bed, he pushed the memories away with the need to put his mouth on her and make her whimper.

Kneeling between her spread thighs, Erik hooked his fingers into the waistband of her panties and slid them down her legs.

"Look how wet you are. For me," he murmured, swiping a finger through the dripping evidence of her arousal. She moaned, her hips chasing after him.

"Please, Erik. Please."

"You're so pretty when you beg, Lola."

Her feet flat on the bed, she bucked up. Her sex was pink and swollen. Pulsing with arousal. The scent of her made him dizzy.

Sweeping in, Erik ran his tongue up her slit, letting the taste of her burst through his mouth. Salty, with a tang he wanted more of.

Finding her clit, he circled around it over and over again, never quite touching it, until her body was strung so tight he thought she might break. And she whimpered again. Only then did he stroke across the tight bundle of nerves.

Her head thrashed back and forth against his pillow. Plunging two fingers deep inside her wet heat, Erik increased the onslaught, drowning in the need to feel her come apart against his mouth.

Her release came on a keening cry. He'd hear about

that in the morning from the other guys, but at the moment he didn't give a good goddamn. Not when her body was clamping hard around his fingers and the gush of her orgasm was filling his mouth.

He worked her through the release, pulling out every last moment of pleasure he could give her. Until she went lax, her body melting into a puddle.

He stroked a hand down her torso, enjoying the way she pushed up into his caress, even with her eyes screwed shut.

"Holy crap," she whispered, her voice scratchy from screaming.

"I'm not nearly done with you, angel," he promised, pushing her tangled hair from her face.

Grabbing his wallet off the top of the table beside them, he fished out the condom he kept in there. Shedding his sweats, he started to roll the condom over his throbbing erection, but she pulled his hands away.

"Let me."

Taking the ring of latex from him, Lola placed it over his head and with slow, torturous movements pushed it down to cover his length. She stayed there once he was covered, stroking up and down in a way that had breath hissing through his clenched teeth.

"I am not going off in your hand, Lola. That's not enough for me. I want all of you."

Her eyes flashed. "You always have. Greedy man."

Oh, she had no idea.

Hooking his arms beneath her knees, Erik moved between her thighs, positioned himself at her opening, and pressed forward.

He pulsed, pushing in a little at a time, both because he didn't want to hurt her and because it felt so damn good. He wanted to savor this moment, draw it out as long as he could.

But Lola wasn't content with that. Her body was already flushing with renewed arousal. Hips matching his. Fingers digging into his ass. She pulled him down to her at the same time she arched up, finally taking all of him.

God, they fit together so well. Always had. He'd never found this with anyone else, and God knew for the first few years he'd tried. But attempting to erase the need for her with other women had been stupid and disappointing.

Because no one could ever measure up.

That was his last coherent thought, because instinct and the red haze of lust took over. He found a rhythm, a familiar one they'd indulged in many times before.

Their mouths and hands raced across sweat-slicked skin. The orgasm built steadily, the pressure of release beckoning him just to let go. But after years of waking up from a sound sleep with memories of Lola leaving him sweaty and hard, he wasn't ready for this to end.

This time, Erik smothered her cry with his mouth, taking even that for himself. The tight grip of her sex sent him careening over the edge. His own orgasm broke across him, consuming everything but the pleasure they'd always found together.

In that vulnerable moment, Erik couldn't stop himself from letting the dam of emotion break free. Everything he'd locked away six years ago rolled over him, a tsunami full of debris and danger.

Realizing too late what a bad idea this was, Erik collapsed onto the bed beside her.

Their labored breaths mingled, harsh in the quiet night. Now that the need had been met, everything else was taking over. The anger and guilt he'd harbored earlier rushed in to steal the pleasure.

Beside him, Lola stirred. Not to roll into him like a lover, but to slip from his bed and reach for her panties on the floor.

And the whole damn mess just got better when he pushed out of bed and reached for the condom to dispose of it. The thing had broken.

With a giant curse, Erik slammed his hand down on the bedside table.

Lola jumped. "What the hell?"

Spinning to look at her, he snatched the busted sleeve of latex from his body and held it up for her to see.

Her eyes went wide with panic.

"Are you on the pill?"

"No." He watched her eyes flash with trepidation. "The timing's close, but I think we should be okay. Are you clean?"

That pissed him off even more. Not because she'd asked—it was a valid question. But because there was a time it wouldn't have been a question at all. It reminded him that she had history he knew nothing about, too. "Why do you think the condom broke? I haven't slept with anyone in over a year. I can't remember how long the thing's been in there."

"And you're just now thinking about this?" Her tone of incredulity scraped down his spine.

"I was a little preoccupied with other things at the time, Lola. I didn't expect to wake up with a naked, willing woman in my bed tonight."

Which reminded him, now that they weren't distracted by hormones and history, to ask what had sent her to his bed.

"What changed, Lola? Why did you come to me tonight?"

A grimace twisted her face. She looked away, crossed her arms over her heavy breasts and then speared him with a level gaze. He knew he wasn't going to like whatever she had to say.

"I wasn't coming to see you, Erik. I was looking for someone else."

"OH, I DEFINITELY got screwed." In more ways than one.

For the second night in a row, Lola found herself at a bar table with her girls clustered around her for moral support.

Only this time she'd insisted on nothing but water. Those damn shots had gotten her into enough trouble already.

No, that wasn't fair. She'd been tipsy, but she'd been fully aware of what she was doing. By the time she realized she'd crawled into Erik's bed instead of Sean's, her libido had taken control and started making the decisions.

Groaning, she said, "I just…couldn't stop." And then

dropped her head onto that table. Because hiding would definitely make everything better.

Tatum snorted. Hope's soothing hand rubbed down her spine. And some blessed soul plopped a brownie onto the table in front of her. The sweet scent of chocolate should have tempted her at least to look up. It didn't.

"It was like no time had passed. Forget how reckless he is. How he nearly got my brother killed. Or the way he just left, breaking up with me by text." She raised her head, looking around the table. "Text! After dating for five years."

What was wrong with her? Six years later she was still so pissed at him. But that hadn't stopped her from wanting him once she'd been in his bed...

She'd told him that she wanted closure. And maybe that was partly true, but there was more. Closure probably should have involved a conversation with words instead of their bodies.

She'd just wanted *him*.

Because she was weak. Once she'd touched him, it had all come flooding back. The first time he'd kissed her, on the front porch of her house with her dad peeking through the blinds. But Erik hadn't cared. He'd wanted her father to know he was taking her seriously. The kiss had been so perfect and sweet, but the expression in his eyes when he'd pulled away...it had slayed her. Crumbled her defenses.

Or the first time they'd made love, late at night by the lake. He hadn't pushed her or expected anything. He'd waited until she was ready and then gave her the most romantic, amazing experience. A hell of a lot better than the first time for most of her friends.

Or the endless, passionate nights they'd shared after. The way he could place his hand on the small of her back and make her feel protected and safe. The expression on his face when he was deep inside her, like she was the only thing on earth worth existing for.

The countless memories that had hurt for six years had suddenly flooded in again, only this time they weren't tinged with pain. Just this wonderful sense of right that she couldn't let go of.

Even if she knew it was temporary.

God, she was pathetic.

Sleeping with him had been a huge mistake. And when she'd told him she'd been looking for someone else, his devastation should have made her feel better. Like she'd given him a little piece of what he'd dished out to her. But it didn't. It made her feel even worse. No matter what had happened between them, she didn't want him to hurt.

Erik had been hurt enough in his life.

"Dammit," she breathed out, rubbing her hands over her gritty eyes. She hadn't slept much last night.

The door opened and raucous laughter followed. Baritone voices boomed above the general din of the place. It was a Wednesday night, but the bar was still plenty busy. Decorated like an Irish pub, it was the comfortable hangout for singles and couples alike in Sweetheart. Dark wood and mellow light gave it a warm, friendly feel even as the high-backed booths offered more privacy than the round table she and the girls occupied.

Lola rolled her head, taking in the group that had just walked in. And immediately straightened.

The last thing she needed was her brother and his phalanx of testosterone-laden friends to see her moping. She just knew word would somehow make it back to Erik. Hell, Colt would probably tell him…if he knew she'd slept with him.

Which she had no intention of ever telling her brother. This was one mistake she planned to keep to herself and her girls.

The group, Colt and Sean among them, pushed through the loitering patrons toward a table at the back of the bar, but they got waylaid when they reached the women.

Gage and Evan slipped up behind their wives, slinging arms around their shoulders or waists. Lola watched Hope and Tatum lean back into their men, a comfortable, familiar gesture that made something in the center of her chest ache.

She'd had that once. Familiarity and comfort. With Erik.

Nope, she wasn't going there. She would not be jealous of her friends and the happiness they'd found.

Lola pushed out her chair, leaving a space for Colt to roll up beside her. "Hey, sis. Didn't realize you were out tonight."

The other guys pulled up chairs, filtering into their group and taking up conversation. Sean squeezed in on her other side, dropping his arm around her shoulders and tangling his fingers into her hair.

She turned and gave him a smile that felt sickly. After what happened last night—and what she'd intended to happen—she was a little uncomfortable with him touching her. It felt wrong for so many reasons. But he wouldn't understand, so Lola left his hand where it was.

Their waitress came by and took orders. The opportunity for conversation with her girls was gone, but Lola didn't mind the camaraderie that replaced it.

These were her people. The ones she could count on to be there for her when she needed them most. Inexplicably, she felt the sting of tears hit her eyes. And out of nowhere, Colt grabbed her hand and squeezed.

She glanced over at him, wishing she hadn't when she realized he was watching her with his calm, steady gaze. For a split second she wondered if he knew. Even growing up, he'd somehow had a sixth sense about when she was headed straight for trouble.

Where'd that skill been last night when she'd needed it?

"You good?" he asked in a soft voice only for her ears.

"No." Because she'd never lie to her brother. Maybe bend the truth or commit the sin of omission, but never outright lie. "I'm pissed at you. Why didn't you tell me he was back?"

"Because I knew you'd just build your armor up that much higher. I don't know what happened between you—I was a little preoccupied and you've never shared the details with me—but I do know it's been holding you back for six years."

"It has not."

His level stare lasered through her. "Lola, you haven't had a real relationship since he left."

"I've dated," she protested. Which was true. Even if none of those dates had led to more than a nice dinner, some pleasant conversation and occasionally a physical outlet. "And I've been busy. It's hard work building a photography business from the ground up."

"Try selling that snake oil somewhere else. I'm the one who books your appointments, sends out your invoices and pays your bills. Your business has been established and highly profitable for the last several years."

She harrumphed.

"Stop using it as an excuse."

She wasn't! Or…crap, maybe she was.

"You guys need to talk things out. Take the opportunity while he's home to get some closure, kid." Colt squeezed her hand again. "So that you can move on with your life and find some happiness."

"I'm happy." She didn't need a man in her life to be happy. Her gaze drifted across the table to Hope and Gage. His arm was around her shoulders as he bent down, murmuring into her ear. The way Hope leaned into him, the expression of bliss on her face… If she were honest with herself, she'd be stupid not to crave that for herself.

The two of them turned back to the conversation flowing around the table. Everyone else ordered another round of drinks, although Lola stuck with her water. Colt gave her a side eye but didn't comment.

They were enjoying themselves. Sean was being charming and funny, telling a story that had the entire table laughing.

But the camaraderie was demolished when about a half hour later, the door slammed open again. Lola's back was to the entrance, but somehow she knew who was coming in before she even turned around.

The shocked, panicked expression on Hope's face was a dead giveaway. Not to mention the way Lola's body reacted. Her muscles tightened with tension and anticipation. Energy crackled across her skin. And she could practically feel those gorgeous gray eyes boring into the back of her neck.

She turned anyway. Yep, he was staring right at her. No, wait, he was staring at Sean and the arm he had wrapped casually over the back of her chair.

Oh, shit.

Colt raised his voice in greeting—"Erik!"—and waved him over.

It was like watching a car accident in slow motion. She could do nothing to stop it, though a warning yelp burst through her lips anyway.

"Erik, don't."

He didn't slow down, just barreled across the bar. Colt's reaction changed, going from welcoming to wary in the space of a second. Unaware of Erik's real target, he rolled his chair backward, effectively blocking Lola in and preventing her from intervening.

Erik's gaze flicked to her for a split second, raking

her with the heat of his anger, but bounding sideways to Sean.

"I've been looking for you," he growled.

Sean, oblivious to the undercurrent, said, "Oh, yeah? What can I do for you?"

Panic seized Lola. She tried to leap over Colt to get to Erik, but only managed to go sprawling over the edge of his chair. Colt's strong hands gripped her, preventing her from flipping headfirst onto the floor.

All she could do was watch in horror.

Fisting his hands into Sean's shirt, Erik jerked him up from his chair. Sean didn't even bother to defend against the first blow, maybe because he hadn't realized it was coming.

But he definitely ducked the second.

3

"LOLA IS NOT the kind of woman you screw around with, you asshole," Erik bit out. He didn't care that half the town was watching, and the other half would know about this fight before he'd managed to clean up his raw knuckles.

Outrage had been building inside him since the moment Lola had walked away last night. Her parting words echoed through his head like the pounding drumbeat of some ancient war chant.

She hadn't been there to see him. She'd been there to see Sean.

Which might not have been a problem, except Sean had been in Charleston to meet up with a woman he was seeing. That was why Erik had been covering his shift.

Gage and Evan moved to intervene, but rubbing his jaw with one hand, Sean held up the other to stop them. He moved into a clearer space so he'd have room to maneuver. Not a complete moron, then.

No, Erik already knew that about Sean. They'd

grown up together, despite the fact the other man was a couple of years younger than him. Sweetheart was a small town, the firehouse even smaller.

Throwing another punch, Erik felt the impact as it reverberated up his arm and into his shoulder. His knuckles burned. It had been a damn long time since he'd gotten into a fistfight.

"You can't play fast and loose with Lola like that. You sure as hell shouldn't be seeing someone else while you're sleeping with her. She's the kind of woman who expects—and deserves—respect and monogamy when she's with a guy."

"Whoa," Sean said, countering with a punch of his own. He could tell the guy was holding back, but it still hurt like hell when Sean's fist connected with the underside of his jaw. Erik's head snapped back.

"Lola and I aren't sleeping together. We flirt and cut up, but she isn't interested in me."

"Erik, stop this. Now," Lola roared.

Neither of them listened, though Sean did back away, his fists dropping just a little. "What in God's name made you think that I'm sleeping with Lola?"

"Because she crawled into your bunk last night half-naked, unaware that I'd picked up your shift."

Lola groaned. Out of the corner of his eye, he saw her sag against Colt's chair. Heat flamed up her face before she buried it in her brother's shoulder. The back of her neck was a matching brilliant shade of red.

"She did what?" Sean asked, genuine shock making his jaw go slack. "Lola…"

She finally looked up at Sean, a sheepish expression

on her face. "So, I had a couple drinks last night and came up with what turned out to be a very stupid idea."

Sean shook his head, clearly dumbfounded. "You aren't really interested in me."

Lola pushed upright, gaining her feet and her composure. Everyone in the place was staring at her, but she didn't seem to care. "No. This really has nothing to do with you, and I'm sorry to drag you into it."

Sean shrugged, rubbing the side of his jaw that would no doubt be sporting bruises tomorrow. "You know I'd help you any way you needed, Lola. And sleeping with you would have been less than a hardship. You're gorgeous and sexy as hell."

Lola's lips quirked. "Thanks. I think."

Erik's hands balled into fists, but Lola's words finally started to sink in, penetrating the fog of outrage that had been building inside him all day. "Wait, you didn't know she was coming to see you?"

"Nope," Sean said.

Erik's narrowed gaze swung to Lola.

She stared at him, her only response a miniscule shrug of her shoulders. "I'm a big girl, Erik. I get to sleep, or not sleep, with whomever I want. Whenever I want. I don't owe anyone an explanation."

Oh, that was where she was damn wrong.

But for the first time since he'd barreled into the bar, he realized—and cared—about the spectacle they were creating.

Because as pissed as he'd been about Sean's supposed treatment of Lola, what he'd just done wasn't much better.

"I'm sorry," he said.

Anger mingling with humor flashed through Lola's gaze. She threw an arm out, taking in the entire bar. "Little late for that, don't you think?"

"Well," Colt said drily, "as much as I've enjoyed the entertainment for the night, I think it's time for everyone to go to their separate corners and chill out for a little while. Erik, why don't you drive me home?"

Erik's gaze dragged reluctantly from Lola down to Colt, the man who had once been his closest friend. The brother he'd never had. But that was long ago. He used to be able to judge this man's moods as quickly as he'd been able to judge Lola's.

Now, both of them were strangers. And he hated that. Colt had lost the use of his legs the night of the accident, and Erik would never forgive himself for his role in that. But he'd lost so much that night, as well. Maybe more.

He'd lost the woman he loved, the brother he'd never had, his surrogate family and the man who'd stepped in and become his father figure.

When everything had happened in California a few weeks ago and he'd found himself on forced leave for two months, the only thing he'd wanted was to come home and lick his wounds.

He should have known that the ones still festering deep inside would just get ripped back open and add to the misery.

Colt's gaze, the same deep brown as Lola's, stared back at him, steady and completely unreadable. For a split second Erik wondered if the other man just wanted to get him alone so he could rip him a new one without an audience.

Not that he didn't deserve it.

"Yeah, okay." Backing up, he gestured for Colt to lead the way. Chairs scraped across the floor behind him, and soft voices murmured. Someone flipped on the music that had stopped after he threw the first punch.

At the door, he couldn't prevent himself from glancing behind him. He wasn't sure whether he wanted her to be watching him leave or ignoring him like he probably deserved. But she wasn't doing either.

Lola was gone.

ERIK STOOD BY, a little helpless, as Colt, using the door and the handle in the ceiling, levered himself up from his wheelchair and into the front seat of Erik's truck. Erik wanted to offer to help, but wasn't sure it would be appreciated.

Besides, it obviously wasn't needed.

Colt pointed to his wheelchair. "Pull up on the seat and it'll fold. Stash it in the back so we can get out of here." He swung around to settle in the passenger seat. "We have some catching up to do."

For the last six years, Erik had worked as a smoke jumper, taking risks and pushing himself to the brink of disaster to fight out-of-control forest fires. Because he could. Because he was damn good at it.

Because he had nothing to lose.

He'd moved around a lot, never settling with one team or in one place. He'd been in Idaho, Washington, Alaska, Montana and, most recently, California.

Up in Flames

Over that time, he'd used the excuse that he was busy to stay away from Sweetheart, coming home mostly at holidays. He'd always managed to avoid Colt and Lola during those trips, telling himself he was there to spend time with his mom anyway.

That was a lie. He hadn't wanted to deal with the accusation he knew would fill their expressions.

The entire drive to his place, Colt kept up a steady stream of conversation. On one hand, it felt like the last six years hadn't even happened and they were right back where they'd always been.

And if he hadn't just picked up the chair Colt was forced to live in, maybe Erik could have pretended. He should have stayed in California. Coming home was a stupid idea.

The pressure of all the words he wanted to say— should have said six years ago—clogged his throat. So Erik sat there, his grip on the steering wheel getting tighter and tighter. Screw his jacked-up knuckles and the pain shooting through his hands. That was nothing compared to what Colt had to live with.

How could he ever ask forgiveness for what he'd cost Colt?

He couldn't.

If Colt noticed Erik's brusque responses, he didn't let on. Erik pulled into Colt's driveway, put the truck in Park and set up his chair outside the open passenger door.

Reaching out, Colt rolled the chair close and then dropped into the seat, repositioning his legs. Colt had always been a strong guy, but even Erik had to marvel at the flex of his biceps.

"Jesus man, what do you bench these days?"

Colt laughed. "More than I used to."

"Obviously." Erik shifted uncomfortably on his feet, about to make his escape. Before he could, Colt started rolling away.

"Get your ass in here and have a beer. And some ice. I bet your hand is throbbing like a bitch."

Erik followed. What else was he supposed to do? "I've had worse."

"Yeah, like the time you wrecked that piece of shit motorcycle you bought off the internet."

God, he'd forgotten about that. It really had been a piece of shit, but he'd planned to repair it. The bike could have been amazing…if he hadn't run it off the road on the way home, smashing it into a tree. He hadn't been seriously injured, but the bike was toast.

Colt, who had been following behind him, picked up the pieces and drove him to the hospital. And he kept the truth from Erik's mom, who hadn't wanted him to buy a bike in the first place.

Those were the days. When he had a brother backing him up. Not that he didn't get along with the guys he worked with now, but it wasn't the same. You couldn't replace the kind of history he'd shared with Colt.

Colt didn't bother stopping to give Erik the grand tour, just wheeled straight to the side-by-side freezer, tossed him a bag of frozen peas without even looking and then snagged two beers.

The peas felt good on the back of his hand. But the cool beer flowing down his throat felt better.

Although he nearly spit the mouthful back out again when Colt said, "This is the point in the evening's entertainment when I tell you to get your head out of your ass."

"Excuse me?"

Colt gave him a pointed stare. "First, whatever you keep thinking when you look at me, forget it. Me being in this chair is not your fault."

"Yes, it is."

"No, it isn't. I made my own choices that night, Erik, knowing full well the risks involved. I agreed to those risks every time I went into a burning building."

"But you shouldn't have been there. You wouldn't have been if I hadn't gone in after Chief gave the order to pull back."

Colt rolled across the kitchen floor, wheels squeaking softly against the hardwood. "Come here."

"What?"

"Come here." He crooked a finger.

With a shake of his head, Erik leaned down and yelped when Colt smacked him in the back of the head.

"What the hell?" he asked, rubbing the spot.

"Someone needs to knock some sense into you. You know me better than that. Always have. If you hadn't gone back into that building, I would have. I wasn't about to leave another boy without a dad if there was something I could do about it. Just like you."

A jolt rocked through Erik. His hands clenched. And a weight he'd been carrying for so long finally…fell away.

"I'm sorry," he whispered. He needed to say the words. Maybe not for Colt, but for himself.

"Yeah, man. I know. What happened sucked, but it was an accident. I've found peace and purpose in it. I'm about to graduate with my master's in psychology. My plan is to help people deal with difficult situations like mine. I'm good. I promise. You, on the other hand, are in a world of trouble."

Wait. Hadn't they just cleared the air?

"What the hell do you think you're doing with my sister?"

With a groan, Erik slumped against the kitchen counter and knocked back a huge gulp from his bottle.

"Nothing. I'm not doing anything with your sister."

"That's not what it sounded like. It *sounded* like you've been home for less than a handful of days and have already managed to get her into bed."

"It wasn't like that."

"Sure, because your dick accidentally slipped, right?"

"Hey! I woke up from a dead sleep to find your sister in *my* bed wearing nothing but a bra and the skimpiest panties on this earth."

Colt made a disgusted sound and ground his palms into his eye sockets. "That's a visual I will never be able to wipe from my brain, asshole."

Erik had to chuckle. This, at least, was familiar territory. This sounded like countless other conversations they'd had about his relationship with Lola. Honestly, there was a part of him that had enjoyed torturing Colt on occasion. So he was human. Whatever.

"Look, I said it back then and I'll say it now. You're both adults, so what you do together is between you guys."

"You say that, but why don't I believe you?"

"Because unlike before, this time I know what's coming—for both of you. What happens when it's time for you to leave town again, Erik? Lola was devastated. You didn't have to watch her waste away for months, heartbroken that you'd left without even really telling her goodbye. You didn't watch the hope she couldn't quite extinguish slowly drive her crazy...until it finally went out altogether. Which, I have to tell you, was ten times worse."

Setting his bottle on the counter, Colt backed away, putting space between them.

"All I'm saying is that you really need to think hard before you act. What do you want? And what's best for Lola? Don't start something with her again if you're not sure you can give it one hundred percent this time. I'm not sure she'd survive the aftermath of you running again. And we both know that these days, running is what you're good at."

Without waiting for his response, Colt rolled away, heading into the back of the house.

Erik had been dismissed.

But Colt's words followed Erik out the door and back to his mom's place. His friend had always been the smart one.

He needed to leave Lola alone. They'd crashed and burned before. Neither of them could survive doing it again.

IT HAD BEEN six weeks since he'd seen Lola. After his talk with Colt, he'd purposely avoided her so he wouldn't make another mistake with her.

The last thing he wanted was to hurt her more than he already had.

Honestly, Colt's words had scared him—a hell of a lot more than parachuting out of a plane into any wildfire he'd faced.

He'd picked up more shifts at the station. A couple of the teams often operated with three men instead of four so it was easy to fill the empty spot, especially when he'd worked with most of the guys before and had a rapport. That history made it easy to blend into a cohesive group.

There were moments when he missed the adrenaline rush of smoke jumping. But with a little distance, he'd realized his chief back in California was right. He'd needed a break. For the last six years he'd been going nonstop. Running from fire to fire in some misguided attempt to make up for what had happened in Sweetheart.

And instead, he'd barreled straight into another tragedy that had cost him a friend and sent him careening into a situation that had almost cost him his own life. Losing Aaron had carried with it a warped sense of déjà vu.

Standing behind Aaron's widow, listening to her muffled sobs, had ripped something open inside him. And he'd taken the bleeding mess straight into another fire and used it to push himself beyond the point of breaking.

Cut off from the team, surrounded by fire with no way out, he'd been lucky. They'd managed to rescue him. He'd been grateful, until Chief had given him the two-month suspension for ignoring orders.

Restless, it had only taken him a few days to realize he needed to be somewhere other than California, watching news stories about a wildfire his team was fighting but he wasn't allowed to touch.

So he'd come home to Sweetheart and walked straight into a history that he'd never actually dealt with. Seeing Lola…it had been like a shot to the gut. He'd wanted her. *Missed* her.

That single night they'd shared wasn't nearly enough. Nothing between them ever had been. Even back when they were dating, he'd felt this overwhelming need to be with her. To touch her. To listen to her talk and rile her up. Lola was so passionate and interesting…he constantly wanted more of her.

Not smart.

Today Erik had come home from an unusually long shift during which he'd barely gotten three hours of sleep, none of them consecutive. They'd been called out on two accidents. In one, a four-year-old child had been trapped inside the twisted metal of a totaled car. Luckily, they'd gotten him out, and from all reports, he had minor injuries and would be fine.

Then, around midnight, they'd gotten a call about smoke coming from the attic in a two-story house just inside the city limits. That one hadn't taken long to extinguish, but before they'd even returned to the station, they were sent back out on a medical call.

Erik had dropped into his bunk and gotten forty-five minutes before a three-alarm apartment fire had come in. That one had kept him up way past time for his shift to end.

He hadn't gotten home until almost 10:00 a.m. and then immediately dropped into sleep. Now it was well past three and he was finally awake. Sort of. His mother was banging something downstairs, the sound of it reverberating through his throbbing skull.

He definitely needed more sleep. Or coffee. Lots of coffee.

Realizing sleep probably wasn't in the cards, Erik pushed up from the bed and tossed on a pair of sweats, not bothering with a shirt. He could smell whatever his mom was cooking, and it was making his stomach rumble. He hadn't eaten in hours.

Shuffling downstairs, he paused in the doorway of the kitchen to find his mom rolling out pie dough. God, he loved his mom's pies. When he was younger he hadn't appreciated all the sacrifices she'd made for him. As a single mom, she'd worked two jobs to provide for him and still somehow managed to have enough energy to do things like bake homemade cookies to include in his lunches and her famous peach pie for Sunday supper.

"Please tell me you aren't taking that to the neighbors or something." Because that was a distinct possibility, and Erik wasn't sure he could deal with the disappointment right now. Not with his head pounding and his body still begging for sleep.

It would be cruel and unusual punishment.

"Of course not. I know you had a rough shift last

night, so I wanted to make your favorite." His mom beamed at him, and a short burst of love mixed with guilt shot through him.

He hadn't been home nearly enough since Colt's accident.

Crossing the kitchen, he wrapped his arms around her and pulled her in for a bear hug. She was a small woman, but somehow he'd never thought of her that way. Not once in his entire life had he heard his mother complain. She always wore a smile, even if it was sometimes lopsided from exhaustion.

"Love you, Mom," he mumbled into the top of her head before stepping back.

"What was that for?" she asked, staring up at him out of her calm, steady eyes, which matched his own.

"Can't I give my mom a hug and tell her I love her?"

"Anytime you want." She offered him a serene smile, turning back to the ingredients spread across the counter. "I've also got a roast in the oven. Everything should be ready in a couple hours. I wasn't sure how long you'd sleep."

"Great. That gives me enough time to fix the faucet upstairs. The handle keeps falling off whenever I turn the water on."

"Yeah. I've been meaning to call someone in to take a look, but there really hasn't been a need since you haven't been home."

Guilt burned through his gut. "I'll deal with it. It'll probably need a new faucet. I can just grab whatever's handy at the hardware store, unless you want to pick it out yourself?"

"Get whatever you think's best." His mom reached out, patting his cheek. "You're a good boy."

"Only because you raised me right."

She laughed, the short burst of sound resonating through his chest and making an answering smile curl his lips.

He'd missed this. Growing up, it had always been the two of them. And while he'd needed to get away from Sweetheart, this trip home was a reminder that he'd run away from more than just Lola, Colt and the accident he couldn't deal with.

A few hours later, he ran to the store and fixed the sink upstairs. After eating the amazing meal his mom had cooked, he even managed to convince her to indulge in watching a movie while he cleaned up, which was where he was when he heard a car pulling into the drive.

He shifted to the front window so he could see who was stopping by.

But that wasn't one of his mom's friends stomping up the front walk.

It was Lola.

What was she doing here?

Erik dried his hands on a towel, tossed it over one shoulder and headed for the front door.

Before he could reach it, she started banging and just kept going, not even giving him a chance to respond.

"What the hell," Erik yelled before he'd even jerked open the front door. The angry expression on her face puzzled him. He hadn't seen her in weeks. What the hell could she be upset about now?

"Lola?"

The screen door was still shut between them. She didn't reach to open it, and for some reason, Erik thought maybe it was smarter to leave that barrier between them for right now.

He was proved right when words burst from her. "You asshole. I'm pregnant."

4

HE HAD TO be hearing things. For a second, Erik thought Lola had said she was pregnant.

And then the expression on her face hit him. Scared, upset, with a mixture of wonder that made his belly clench.

Realization barreled into him. He'd heard her correctly. And that tiny kernel of wonder sprouted in his own belly…for about five seconds. Right up until she spun on her heel and stormed down his mom's front steps.

That was it. She'd dropped her bomb, broke apart his world and was just planning to leave.

Not on your life.

Erik didn't even stop to think. He slammed open the door, and it bounced off the side of the house with a resounding bang. He was across the wide veranda with her arm in his hand as he spun her.

"What?"

"You heard me," she ground out.

Yes. Yes, he had. He opened his mouth to say something, but his head was spinning so fast that he had no idea what.

Their night together was etched into his brain, and not just because of the broken condom. The last six weeks had been sheer hell. Every place he seemed to go in Sweetheart was filled with memories of Lola. And when he wasn't fighting the pull of their history while he was awake, the pulsing frenzy of their night together twisted through his dreams, jolting him awake, making him ache for her.

But he'd listened to Colt and stayed away because it was the right thing to do for Lola.

This changed everything.

"You aren't going to ask me if it's yours?"

The sneer in her words hurt, which was exactly why she'd said them. But what pissed him off more than the petty slash was the implied cut to herself.

"No, Lola. That never even crossed my mind. You wouldn't be here if you didn't know the baby was mine. And you've never slept around."

"You don't know anything about me anymore. I could sleep around."

"But you don't." People didn't change that much, not at their core.

"I was sneaking into someone else's bed that night."

God, he really wished she'd stop reminding him. "I'm aware. I'm also aware that you never actually slept with Sean."

"But I could have."

"No, you couldn't have." He might have avoided Lola

over the past several weeks, but he hadn't avoided Colt. And while his friend had been quick to warn him away from Lola, he hadn't shied away from talking about her.

Erik was well aware that she'd rarely dated over the last six years, and never the same guy more than once or twice. Her love life sounded as interesting as his own. He hadn't been a saint, but he hadn't exactly been filling his phone with random numbers, either.

"We need to talk," he said. Lola tried to jerk away from him, but he kept a firm grip on her arm. Her shoulder sagged a little beneath the weight of the fear she couldn't quite hide.

He wanted to banish it for her. But that wasn't his place anymore.

Finally she sighed. "I know, but I'm not ready for this."

Erik wasn't sure if she meant their discussion or being pregnant. Not that it really mattered. They were going to have to deal with both. And the conversation was going to start now.

Erik led her back up onto the wraparound porch and guided her to the swing at the far end, his hand nestled against the small of her back. The gesture was comfortable and familiar, a feeling of rightness in the middle of a storm.

He settled her and then took several steps away, leaning his hip against the porch railing.

Crossing his arms over his chest, he watched her for several seconds. Lola Whittaker had always been beautiful. Wild and willful, with a creative bent that astounded him because he didn't have a creative bone in his body. Growing up, she was always making, painting or gluing something or other. Or else she had a camera in her hand.

At first it had been an old film camera that her mom had kept. And then, after he'd worked six months to save enough, the top-of-the-line digital camera he'd bought for her because he knew she wanted to study photography at the art college in Charleston and wouldn't ask her dad for the newer equipment.

He'd given the camera to her for Christmas her junior year of high school because she needed it and he'd wanted to give her that. She deserved happiness and dreams. She deserved everything—then and now. The bonus had been her finally agreeing to go out with him after she'd opened the box. That wasn't why he'd done it, but...

She was tamer now, but he could still see her wildness lurking beneath the surface, even in the subtle streaks of teal and blue that whispered through her dark brown hair. They hadn't been there a few weeks ago.

He hated to think he'd been even partly responsible for dulling any of that edge. Her passion and self-assurance were two of the things he'd always admired about her. She didn't hold back, no matter what.

At the moment, her fingers were wrapped around the edge of the seat, as if she was just waiting for a reason to vault up and sprint away.

"I don't expect anything from you," she finally declared.

"Well, that's a shitty thing to say."

"No, it isn't. It's an honest thing to say. We both

know your life is in California now, Erik. I don't know. Maybe you have a girlfriend or fiancée or something."

"That's an even shittier thing to say, and you know it. I never would have slept with you that night if I'd had anyone else in my life. You're beautiful and I've always wanted you, but I have integrity and willpower and the ability to exercise both."

Lola folded in on herself, pulling one foot up onto the swing and hugging her knee. Her gaze dropped to the floor and she blew out a harsh breath. The motion of it fluttered her bangs into her eyes. Erik's fingers itched to reach out and swipe them away so he could see what she was thinking.

"Yeah, you're right." She glanced up at him from beneath her lashes. "That was a low, undeserved blow and I'm sorry. You've never been that guy, and I know it."

"Yes, you do."

"I'm just…" Her foot dropped to the ground, and her head fell back so that she was staring up at the first hint of the moon pushing into the summer sky. The old swing creaked as she toed the ground and sent it rocking. "…floundering a bit, I guess. This came out of left field."

"I bet."

Straightening, she speared him with a steady gaze. "I meant it. I don't expect anything from you. I have a great job and can support our child just fine. I needed to tell you, though. The right thing was to tell you. I mean, I only took the test—" she glanced at her watch "—thirty minutes ago."

He had no idea what it meant that she'd hopped

straight into her car and come to tell him. Maybe nothing other than Lola possessed as much integrity as he'd just claimed to have.

"Lola, you know what my childhood was like better than most. Do you really think I'd walk away from my child?"

Lola's eyes went wide with surprise and a bit of guilt. "No, of course not." Her tone emphatic, she said it again. "No. That's not what I meant. Of course you'll be a part of the baby's life. However much you want to be involved. But the reality is, we'll be here and you'll be there."

If it was possible, her eyes went even rounder. "And for God's sake, do not get some harebrained notion of falling on your sword over this. I will personally murder you if you even mention the *m* word. There is no 'do the right thing' here, got it?"

An unexpected bark of laughter shot through him. "The *m* word?"

Groaning, Lola pushed up from the swing and settled against the railing beside him. Her hand brushed against his for the briefest second before she scooted an inch away. A glimpse of the familiarity they used to share.

There was a time Lola had known him intimately—and he was talking more than just physically. Her brother had been his best friend, and even Colt didn't know some of the things he'd shared with Lola.

Erik missed that connection. And that brief, almost nonexistent brush of her fingers against him was a sharp reminder of just what his life was missing.

"You know what I mean." She sighed. "Look, you're

a good guy and I've always known you'd be a great dad. But...there's too much bad history between us to make this anything more than it is. I will not manufacture something that isn't there for the sake of a kid. That's not fair to anyone involved. This has happened and we'll figure out how to deal with it. For all of us."

"You're being quite practical." Which should have made him feel steady and calm. Instead, a sudden nervous energy was sparking beneath his skin. Like he needed to *do* something, but he had no idea what.

"That's me. You know I tackle problems head-on. Always have. When do you go back, anyway?"

"Huh?" Erik's brain was still spinning, so it took him a few seconds to follow Lola's train of thought. "Oh, I planned to stay for another couple weeks."

"Great." She cut her eyes at him. "Part of me wants to know why you're here when there's a fire raging in California right now, but I'm not going to ask because it's none of my business."

No, it wasn't. He wasn't ready to share about Aaron's death and everything that had come afterward. Not even with Lola.

She waited for a few seconds, but when it was obvious he wasn't going to answer her backhanded question, she shrugged. "We have plenty of time to talk about logistics before you head home. Give me your phone."

"What?"

Holding out her hand, Lola waggled her fingers. "Phone."

Pulling it from his pocket, Erik unlocked his screen and handed it over. He watched as she entered her contact information. "Give me a call in a couple days and we'll have lunch. Talk."

Before he could even move, she was darting past him and down the steps again.

"Wait," he called, jogging after her.

She paused at the bottom, surrounded by the rosebushes he'd watched his mom pour countless hours into. Her honey-toned skin was radiant in the final rays of sunshine. Her eyes were bright and clear. And he didn't want her to leave.

"Are you feeling okay?"

Shrugging, she tossed him a brilliant smile. "I've been really tired. Thought it was from the flu, although I guess that wasn't true."

"You need to take care of yourself. And the baby."

Holy shit. Lola was having his baby.

Erik grasped the newel post on the railing. His knees were suddenly shaking and he didn't trust them to hold him up.

Lola was handling this so calmly, while he was starting to feel like the ground was moving beneath his feet, about to swallow him.

GOD, THIS WAS going to be the hardest thing she'd ever done.

Not becoming a mom. After the initial shock, Lola couldn't quite suppress the effervescent happiness that suffused her.

The next day Lola sat in the large office in her studio and stared out the window, her mind whirling.

No, the situation wasn't ideal. Would she have preferred to be happily married with a man who loved her before she had a baby? You bet. But she was so excited at the prospect of having a little life to nurture and watch grow.

She'd left Erik's place and immediately gone to see her dad. His support had been overwhelming, but she'd always known it would be. She was an adult and could easily support herself and her child. Her dad was thrilled at the prospect of becoming a grandpa.

Colt was another story. Oh, he'd pretended to be happy for her, but he couldn't hide his anger with Erik. He wasn't upset that she was pregnant, but that she was pregnant with Erik's baby. Which wasn't really fair, all things considered.

What bothered her most was that Colt and Erik had appeared to put the past behind them over the last few weeks, which she was grateful for. Immediately following the accident, Colt had been angry with everyone and everything—something his psychologist had told them was normal.

That phase hadn't lasted long, but Erik had definitely been the source of a few furious outbursts. The reaction had faded long before Erik had come home, and Lola knew they'd been spending time together, even if she didn't know exactly what they'd talked about.

She'd argued with Colt that it had taken both of them to get pregnant and reminded her brother that she'd been the one to climb into Erik's bed—even if saying the words had embarrassed the hell out of her.

She wasn't sure they'd made much difference.

But that was something she couldn't worry about right now.

She'd been reviewing shots from a session she'd done with a mom and her newborn several weeks ago. The realization that this time next year she'd be holding her own baby had sent her into a state of wonder.

Colt was working at his desk on the other side of hers. At first, she'd given him a space of his own, but that had been impractical. They'd just ended up yelling at each other across the hall. Besides, her office was more than big enough to share.

"Earth to Lola."

"Huh?" Shaking her head, she looked over at her brother. "Sorry. I was…thinking."

"You wanna tell me what put that faraway look and dreamy glaze in your eyes?"

"Not particularly."

Colt harrumphed but didn't push. "As I said about three times while you were ignoring me, I've confirmed with Misty Wilson for her wedding on Saturday. Everything is pretty standard."

"Great."

"Are you sure you're up to this? It's a huge wedding and long reception. You'll probably be on your feet for ten to twelve hours."

"We are not having this conversation." *Again.* "I'm perfectly capable of working. I'm pregnant, not sick. It's going to be a long seven months if you question my ability to do my job every time I take on a client. Don't make me fire you."

Colt harrumphed again, a frown beetling the spot between his eyebrows. "Excuse me for being concerned."

God, her brother was a master at the guilt trip. Probably because he'd learned it from their mother.

"Nope, not starting that, either. I appreciate your concern. Really, I do. And I love you, you big lug. But here you're my employee, not my brother. You have to save the big brother card for outside these walls."

"Yeah, right. We both know that ain't happening, princess."

Lola was about to argue more, but the chime on her phone stopped her. She didn't recognize the number on the screen.

"Hello?"

"Lola."

The riot of emotions that tangled in her belly at the mere sound of Erik's voice tied her in knots. God, this wasn't good.

How was she supposed to raise a child with him if her body revolted whenever he spoke? She needed to get a hold of herself. Now. Before she did something stupid—like sleep with him again and heap even more complications onto an already difficult situation.

On the bright side, she couldn't accidentally get pregnant twice.

"Erik."

Across from her, Colt leaned out from behind the screen of his computer, not even pretending not to eavesdrop.

Lola shooed him away, which didn't work.

"I wanted to set up that lunch date you mentioned so that we could talk."

"We both know it won't be a date, but I do agree we

need to come up with a plan. Or at least get an idea of what we're both thinking."

Glancing up, her gaze snagged on Colt. At least his nosiness would come in handy. "Make yourself useful and look at my calendar, would you? Tell me when I have some time around lunch to meet with Erik."

Colt's gaze narrowed, but he scooted back behind his monitor. "You have about two hours free tomorrow between the Miller family's session and the newborn portraits for baby Jacobs."

Perfect. She liked having a finite time. An exit strategy was always a good thing, especially where Erik was concerned.

"I can meet tomorrow," she told Erik. "Let's say eleven thirty at…" She tried to think of somewhere busy, but not so busy that they'd be surrounded by people who would make as much effort to pretend they weren't listening as Colt was.

"Rosie's," they both said at the same time.

It shouldn't have sent a little zing through her chest that he'd come to the same conclusion she had.

"Great. I'll see you then."

Punching the end button, Lola gently set her phone face down on her desk. Her head was a mess, and not just because they were going to need to tackle some pretty heavy subjects tomorrow.

Every time she saw Erik, it was like a punch to the gut. A reminder of everything she'd had and lost. The sound of Colt's wheels rubbing against the hardwood floor pulled her focus back where it needed to be.

He rolled up beside her and stared for several seconds. Her brother had always had this way of looking at you that made you think he was dissecting your mind, noticing everything you were trying to hide.

And his uncanny ability had only gotten more intense since his accident. It was like his freaking superpower. On more than one occasion, Lola had found herself filling his heavy silences with confessions she'd never had any intention of making.

It was a quality that would make him a good therapist when he finished his coursework.

"You okay?" he eventually asked.

She shrugged. She could lie and tell him yes, but he already knew the answer or he wouldn't have been asking.

"I'm not saying this won't be difficult. He broke my heart, Colt."

"I know. I was there."

"But I'm pretty sure he broke his own, too, so I can't really be pissed about it. Or I can, but that anger is tempered with a healthy dose of regret and sadness. The bottom line is, I refuse to let our baby pay for our mistakes."

"So, what are you going to do?"

"Take the next couple weeks and figure out how to be friends. I mean, we were always that, right? Even before we were lovers, we were friends."

"Please, for the love of God, don't ever use the word *lovers* with me again."

Lola flicked a paper clip at her brother's head, satisfied when it bounced harmlessly off his crown.

"I'm not picking that up, brat."

"Whatever. We'll figure it out. Because we really don't have any other options. No matter what else he might be, there's no doubt Erik will be an amazing dad."

"When he's here," Colt mumbled beneath his breath, but not low enough that she wouldn't hear.

A twinge of fear chased up her spine. Her brother had given voice to one of her biggest concerns.

"You know what he's been doing for the past six years, Lola. A few months here. An assignment there. The longest he's been anywhere is California, and whatever happened there has sent him running back here. He runs. Are you sure he won't do that with the baby?"

No, she wasn't. Not entirely. But she also knew that he'd been abandoned by his own father and sported those scars deep inside. On quiet nights when they'd talked, Erik had opened up to her about how difficult growing up without his dad had been. Her own dad had stepped in, filling that role for Erik in a way that had engendered a bit of hero worship. She wasn't oblivious enough to ignore her father's influence on Erik's career choice.

Erik might not want to act like his own father now, but Lola didn't have the heart to point out that he'd pretty much already done that by running away six years ago.

Still… "As sure as I can be. I'm not blind to his faults, Colt, but I don't think he'll abandon his child. And deep down, you don't, either. I think maybe that's why you're so pissed at him…because he won't walk away even if that might be easier for me. And maybe the baby."

"No, I'm pissed because he's an inconsiderate idiot who got my sister pregnant when he had no intention of seeing a relationship through. In a few weeks he'll go back to his life, Lo, and leave you here with the baby. He'll pop in now and again, no doubt bringing presents and playing the perfect dad before disappearing again. Once again, dodging responsibility."

"Now, wait just a second. You don't think that, not really. I get that you're upset about this, but you're putting all the blame on him, Colt, which isn't fair."

Sleeping with Erik had clearly been a mistake that neither of them needed to repeat. If she hadn't gotten pregnant, they could have pretended that the night never happened.

Lola picked up another paper clip, unbending it absently. "I used to daydream about what he'd be like with our kids. At least now I don't have to wonder."

Giving her brother an unhappy smile, she said, "Life has a strange way of answering prayers in the most unexpected ways, huh?"

"Absolutely." Reaching for her hand, Colt squeezed before letting go. "Would you like a little advice?"

Lola raked her gaze across her brother, her mouth pulling into a wry grimace. "Probably not, but you're going to give it to me anyway, aren't you?"

"Yep. Decide what you want and stand firm. You need to set the tone and expectations here. And whatever you do, don't let yourself get wrapped back up in his life, Lola."

She rubbed her hands over her face. Colt wasn't telling her anything she hadn't already told herself. Her biggest fear right now was that spending any time with Erik would bring up old emotions and make them feel new and exciting. "Erik is larger than life. Always has been. I'm so afraid that I'm not going to be able to resist him, Colt. I've never been able to tell him no. Hello, that's pretty much how I ended up here."

"Ugh, Lo. Haven't we talked about this before? I do *not* want details."

She smacked at his arm. "This baby wasn't a miraculous conception, dingbat. But that night proved one thing. Nothing has changed. We still have chemistry and a physical connection that's off the charts. But Erik's not just a firefighter now. He's a smoke jumper. He left here and found an even more dangerous line of work. Something that could take his life in the blink of an eye."

Colt sighed. "Yeah. I heard one of the guys he worked with died in a fire a couple months ago."

Lola sucked in a harsh breath, wondering if that had anything to do with Erik's sudden appearance here in Sweetheart. Her chest ached at the thought.

Anytime she heard about a community losing a firefighter she couldn't help but think of the danger her brother and father had faced. That Erik still faced. Somehow, over the years those thoughts had become tangled with the reality of losing her mom.

Her sudden hit of grief must have telegraphed all over her face because Colt said, "Losing Mom hit you hard."

"It hit us all hard, but yeah." She'd been young, thirteen. Old enough to remember her mom with that childlike worship that never matured into respect and understanding—what she shared with her dad. Young enough to feel the void that had never been filled.

She'd always lived with the reality that she could lose her father whenever he walked out the door. To then have her mother—the constant stability in her life—yanked away from her so suddenly and violently—well, she didn't need a shrink to understand the psychological scars.

When her father had taken the job as chief, some of that residual fear had subsided. Until Colt and Erik joined. Then Colt's accident had happened, and Erik had up and left.

Yeah, she wasn't anywhere close to ready to contemplate giving their relationship a second chance. Especially because of a baby. That was a really terrible reason to jump into any relationship.

"I know what you're worried about," she said, "and it isn't going to happen. If Erik had wanted a second chance, he could have asked for it at any point. He's been here for six weeks. Instead, I haven't heard from him since the night we were together."

A sheepish expression crossed Colt's face. "Yeah, well, that might have been my fault."

"What did you do?" she asked, each word slow and deliberate.

"Nothing. Well, nothing that didn't need to be done. I just gave him a gentle warning about playing with your emotions."

Lola groaned. "I really wish you'd stop meddling in my life."

Reaching out, Colt ruffled her hair. "Never gonna

happen. That's pretty much in the job description. You'd think you'd be used to it by now."

"Fat chance. You do realize I'm an adult."

Giving her a brilliant grin, Colt started rolling backward, his only answer a shrug that had her searching for another paper clip.

5

GOD WAS NOT answering any prayers today, good, bad or completely off the wall. Lola was running late thanks to the smallest Miller, who decided to spew fruit punch and Goldfish crackers all over her, her equipment and her favorite studio sofa. The vintage blue velvet one with the intricately carved feet.

Luckily, early sessions involving small children and nervous brides holding glasses of wine had taught her to have backup clothes available at all times. Colt was currently on the phone with a restoration company scheduled to come out and clean the sofa. And after a quick swipe of a damp cloth, her equipment was fine and functional.

But she was tired, queasy and sweating.

Unless Lexi was dragging her out for a run or to the gym, she hated to sweat.

She was sticky, frazzled and definitely in less than an ideal state of mind when she pushed open the door to Rosie's.

The scent of marinara sauce, sourdough bread and Italian sausage smacked her in the face. How could she be both starving and nauseated at the same time?

Spotting Erik in a booth toward the back of the restaurant, she gestured to the hostess and then weaved through the tables.

"I was beginning to think you'd stood me up," he said, getting to his feet as she approached and slid into the booth.

"The thought might have crossed my mind, but it wouldn't have accomplished anything, so… I'm running behind because I had a small disaster with a tiny human during my last session." Ironically, that probably should have made her give this motherhood thing a second thought, but it hadn't.

"Do I want to know?"

"Not if you plan to eat anything with red sauce on it. Or, anything at all, really."

Erik raised a single eyebrow but kept his lips firmly sealed.

"Smart man." Their waiter had brought out a plate of bread and a little saucer with olive oil and herbs. She noted that Erik already ordered a sweet tea for her. She'd been drinking the stuff practically out of her baby bottle.

The fact that he remembered what she preferred to drink after so many years shouldn't have made her smile, but it did.

She tore off a hunk of bread, sopped it through the oil and shoved it into her mouth. On the bright side, thanks to years of being comfortable with each other, she didn't care one whit what Erik thought of her eating habits. "I'm starving." Her uncooperative belly had settled down.

Ripping off more bread, she took another bite and slowly raised her gaze up to Erik's. He was watching her, an enigmatic expression on his face.

There was a time where she'd known every single nuance of this man, but now she had no idea what he was thinking. And wasn't in the right frame of mind to ask.

Their waiter came by and took their order, giving her a few minutes to find her equilibrium after everything that had happened today. Sitting back into the soft cushions of the booth, Lola asked, "What are your thoughts?"

"On what? The political climate? The weather we're having? Who's going to win the World Series this year?"

"Very funny. You're a laugh a minute. On our baby."

Something sharp passed through his gaze. It was there and gone before she could pinpoint or analyze.

"I'm not sure I have many."

Lola couldn't decide if that was a good or bad thing. Would he be open to her thoughts on visitation and co-parenting, or was he simply getting the lay of the land first?

"Well, I know that I plan to breast-feed."

"That's good. Everything I've read suggests that's best for the baby. At least in the beginning."

Everything he'd read?

"Have you been planning on kids with someone

else?" The question was out, bypassing her filter before she could even form the thought that she shouldn't ask.

"No. I already told you I'm not seeing anyone. I haven't seen anyone even semiseriously for a year or so."

Semiseriously? What the heck was that supposed to mean?

And a year or so. She couldn't quite kill the part of her that wanted to hunt down whomever he'd been seeing *then* and rip the hair from her head. No, she didn't normally struggle with violent reactions. Yes, she realized she had no right to be jealous. But there it was.

At least she was smart enough not to voice the impulse.

"Well, I suppose that's good," she said. "For you, anyway. Kinda difficult to explain going to visit your mom and coming home a daddy-to-be."

His droll expression had her biting back a laugh. "I bought a book last night and started reading," he said. "I do not recommend you buy the book, unless you want to be awake all night worrying about pregnancy complications and childhood illnesses, but it was…insightful."

He'd bought a book. Last night. And from the sounds of things, had stayed up most of the night reading it. What the hell was she supposed to do with that?

Shaking her head, Lola said, "Noted. Anyway, so it won't be practical for the baby to visit you in California probably for at least the first year. I mean, yeah, I could pump and send milk, but that's a lot to store. I'd like to ask that you come back to Sweetheart, at least in the beginning."

He frowned. "Why don't you both come to California?"

"Because I have a business to run, one that doesn't bring in any revenue if I'm not here working."

"I'll take care of you both."

The urge to reach across the table and smack him upside the head was strong. She should have won brownie points for resisting.

"You know me better than that. I'm not the kind of girl who'd be happy being taken care of."

"I know." His rueful tone rubbed her the wrong way.

"What's that supposed to mean?"

"Nothing. I don't want to fight about something that doesn't matter anymore."

But that implied something *had* mattered once. Yet he'd never bothered to tell her.

And now she wanted to know. *Needed* to know. She was surely some kind of masochist.

"Oh, no, you don't," she said. "You started this. Part of getting to the point of being friends is going to involve dealing with what happened between us. So spit it out. Clear the air."

Erik shook his head, his mouth pulling down into a frown. "This is a bad idea."

"I disagree."

"And that, right there, was always a problem. You are a strong woman, Lola. Always have been. One of the things that drew me in was your fire and confidence. From the time you were a little girl, you had that spark.

"But you're also bullheaded and blind to anyone

else's way of thinking. It never occurs to you that someone could see the world other than the way you do."

That wasn't true, was it? Lola sputtered, "I don't…"

Erik's expression softened. "You do. You're a force to
be reckoned with when you've got a cause or a goal. It's
amazing to watch, as long as I'm not the one standing in
your path, about to be bowled over. Your dedication and
determination are inspiring and intimidating at the same
time. You're infectious. I'll never forget your sophomore
year when you decided to organize a coat drive because
you'd seen a news story about the homeless population
in Charleston. I've always known you would accomplish amazing things. And I've always known you didn't
need me—or anyone—in order to do that."

Jesus. She'd thought her heart had been broken years
ago when Erik walked away. Shattered and mended.
She'd been wrong. Somehow, his words today had managed to shatter her all over again. They hurt in a way
she was pretty sure he hadn't meant for them to.

Didn't change the fact that they did.

"You idiotic man. I might not have needed you in
order to be successful, but I sure as hell wanted you
standing next to me. You left when I needed you most,
Erik. I was devastated, going through the second worst
experience of my life, and the man I thought would
stand beside me through anything was just…gone."

All the emotions she'd fought during the days and
weeks following Colt's accident and Erik's disappear-
ance surfaced again, hot and caustic. Anger and disappointment burned through her gut.

She wanted to yell at him, to let loose all the things

she'd screamed at her bedroom walls in the middle of the night. But that wouldn't solve anything right now. Instead, she swallowed the emotions back down…just like she'd been doing for six years.

Old habits were hard to break.

"You're right, this was a bad idea," she said through gritted teeth. "It isn't the time or the place."

"No. We should have had this conversation years ago."

Ha! "Probably before you uprooted and left with barely a goodbye and no explanation."

Erik had thrown away their relationship of five years. And that was something she wasn't willing to forget.

"Lola. I…couldn't stay. I couldn't watch him suffer. I couldn't watch you struggle."

"Right. That's bullshit, and we both know it. You couldn't deal with your guilt."

His head dropped and he whispered, "You're right."

The admission should have made her feel…something. Vindication. Justification. Instead, she felt hollow. Because his admission changed absolutely nothing.

"You think I don't know Colt's accident was entirely my fault?" he went on. "That I don't live every single day with the knowledge that I cost my best friend his legs, his career and any chance at a family?"

Erik's palms slammed down onto the table, rattling plates and silverware. "Do you think I wouldn't give everything I have to trade places with him? I'd do anything to fix what I broke, Lola."

He stared at her across the table, his stormy gray eyes a swirling mass of emotions that made her chest ache. She wanted to reach out and soothe him. She also wanted to hurt him the way he'd made her hurt for years.

But she did neither. Instead, Lola sat there, unblinking. Waiting. For something that could never happen. Because no one could go back in time and fix what had happened.

They were at a stalemate, neither of them knowing what to do or say. Silence stretched between them. Nausea rolled through Lola's belly. Finally she murmured, "Now what?"

Erik shrugged. "We deal with what's in front of us instead of what we can't change from the past." Erik picked up her hand and threaded her fingers through his. "We can figure this out, Lola. Together."

God, she hoped he was right. For the baby's sake if not for their own.

But she had her doubts.

Being around Erik was...confusing. She wanted to hate him. A part of her really did. But she couldn't stop caring about him.

Which was exceedingly stupid. She needed to be careful not to let herself get attached to Erik again. They were going to share a child, nothing more. She'd given him her heart once and he'd handed it back.

He'd run away and spent the last six years wandering from job to job, place to place, never settling anywhere. Erik was reckless and restless, two things she couldn't afford even if a baby weren't involved.

She needed to remember that she couldn't rely on

Erik. She'd counted on him once. She wasn't going to make that same mistake again.

THE BELL OVER the door of Bliss Photography tinkled when Erik opened it.

He'd driven by Lola's studio numerous times since he'd been home. Right on Main Street, it was hard to miss. Like the other stores along the street, the building had an old-world, homey feel, with intricate woodwork along the eaves and two amazing displays of her photos in the windows.

Inside were even more examples of Lola's talent. Huge canvases of kids and babies. Families and brides. Even a few landscapes. He wasn't much of a judge of art, but her work was amazing. He'd always thought so. She'd only gotten better over the years. Her ability to capture people in a way that made them beautiful and human at the same time was a talent he admired.

His boots echoed off the hardwood floors as he walked down the hallway, glancing to the left and right, taking in the props and wide-open studio space. There was an expectant silence, almost like Lola's studio was waiting for the laughter and noise that would bring it to life when clients joined the party.

God, what he wouldn't give to see her in action.

"Come on back," Colt's voice rang out from somewhere in the rear.

Erik headed toward the only open doorway with light spilling out.

"Hey, man," Erik called. "Still speaking to me? Or do I need to brace for an ass-kicking?"

Over the last few weeks he and Colt had picked up their friendship. After that first night, neither of them had mentioned the accident or what had happened six years ago. Colt had apparently said all he'd wanted to on the subject, and Erik wasn't ready to rip into his own thoughts just yet.

Maybe he was more of a coward than he'd ever realized.

He had to admit, it had been wonderful to have his best friend back, even temporarily. Sure, he had friends that he hung with, and even one in California that he'd become pretty close to. But he and Colt had been friends since they were ten. There was just no replacing that kind of history.

Colt knew everything about him. Or he used to.

And it bothered Erik now to wonder if his rash actions with Lola were going to cost him this fledgling reunion. He wouldn't blame Colt for being pissed. Hell, if he had a sister who'd accidentally gotten pregnant... yeah, he'd have bloodied his knuckles on the guy's face long before now.

Colt jerked his chin up in a distracted greeting. With a final glance at the computer screen, he pushed away from the desk. Erik loitered in the doorway, and for several seconds he simply let the question hang in the air, unanswered.

He fully expected to get a verbal beat down from Lola's brother. But after debating the merits of letting Colt's temper cool or getting the punishment over with, he'd decided better to take a page from Lola's book and deal with the situation head-on.

Arms crossed over his chest, Colt glared at him. "You definitely deserve an ass-kicking, but Lola's pretty capable of doing that herself, so I won't bother."

Well, that was a small relief. He really didn't want to fight a guy in a wheelchair.

"Am I happy with what's happening? Hell, no. Erik, you weren't here to see how devastated she was when you left. I have to admit that I was happy to see you back off after that first night we talked. It was the right thing to do. But now..." Colt shook his head.

"It's a clusterfuck." It was a relief to say it out loud. He hadn't said that to Lola. He'd wanted to appear strong and confident for her.

"Oh, you've got that right. You two both have some major decisions to make and now, no matter what, you'll be involved in each other's lives forever."

The way Colt said it made clear he didn't think that was a good thing. Which hurt more than Erik wanted to admit. Sure, over the years Colt had given him shit about dating his little sister. But he'd never once told Erik he wasn't good enough for Lola.

And now Erik wasn't good enough for Colt's sister *or* for the niece or nephew on the way.

A part of Erik even agreed. He was scared out of his ever loving mind. But he'd never admit it.

Instead, he projected a sense of calm he was far from feeling. "We'll figure it out, man. I loved your sister, but more than that, I respect her. She's always been strong and confident. Known exactly what she wanted and had a plan to get it. She's going to be an amazing mom."

"On that, at least, we agree."

An uncomfortable silence filled the space between them. Erik shifted on his feet, jangling the change in his pockets. "So...where is she?"

Colt narrowed his eyes before slowly answering. "Home. Today wasn't a good day. I rescheduled her afternoon appointments and chased her out."

It went without saying that Colt had most likely done this without actually consulting her. Both men knew she wouldn't have willingly rescheduled a client unless she was passed out or in the hospital. Stubborn woman.

Part of Erik was disappointed to miss the fireworks—no doubt Lola fought him every step of the way as her brother escorted her out of the building.

God, the woman could be so frustrating. But he didn't like hearing she wasn't feeling well. He was surprised to find himself upset that she hadn't told him.

Logically he knew she didn't have any requirement to let him know. But she was carrying his baby, and it felt like he should be taking care of her. She'd never let him, though, even if they'd been in a relationship. Which they weren't.

God, this was frustrating and complicated.

Now that he thought of it, there was something he could do. Something concrete he could focus on, instead of the unanswered questions. Like how they were going to handle the logistics of coparenting.

Or how they were going to find their way back to being friends, at least.

Flipping a wave, Erik said, "Later," and walked out the door. Colt's grumble followed him, but Erik couldn't muster up the energy to care what he was saying.

He made a couple of stops along the way, and twenty minutes later, he was standing on Lola's front porch, his arms filled with supplies.

Erik juggled everything, managing to knock softly.

It didn't take long before Lola was standing in the middle of the open doorway, staring up at him out of heavy-lidded eyes. Her face was pale beneath the honey tone of her skin and clean of any makeup. Her hair was pulled onto the top of her head in a messy knot that had straggling curls trailing down her neck. She wore the tiniest pair of athletic shorts and a tank top that clung to every curve of her body.

God, how could she look so edible and miserable at the same time?

"Now is not a good time, Erik. Go away." She didn't bother to wait before trying to shut the door in his face. He was fast enough to wedge a foot in and stop it from closing.

"Wait. I come bearing gifts. Colt told me you weren't feeling well." Pushing past her, Erik walked into her house. He went straight to the kitchen counter jutting into the open living room and let his pile of goodies cascade down. "I wasn't sure what would work so I brought a little of everything—saltines, ginger ale, chicken noodle soup, popsicles, pickles—"

"Pickles?" The expression on her face suggested that one had been a bad decision.

He shrugged. "I figured if you didn't want them now, maybe you would later." Turning, he took her in. She hesitated, halfway across the room and hovering beside the closed front door like she was just waiting for a reason to usher him out again.

"I also picked up a couple movies. Something to maybe take your mind off things."

She huffed, but didn't immediately tell him to leave.

So he decided to press his luck. "Why didn't you call me?"

"About what?"

"To tell me you weren't feeling well."

"Because it isn't your problem."

Erik sighed. They had very different ideas about how this was going to work. Crossing to her, he grasped her shoulders, ducked until he was looking her straight in the eyes and said, "Yes, it is. You're pregnant with my child, Lola. That means something to me."

Her frown didn't give him the warm fuzzies. "I hear you."

"Apparently you don't. We might not be together, but you aren't dealing with this alone. Any of it. If you're sick, I want to know."

Jerking her gaze away, Lola tried to pull out of his hold, but he tightened his grip, keeping her right where she belonged. Maybe she wasn't ready to hear his words, but that wouldn't stop him from showing her that he really meant them.

Erik turned her around, led her over to the sofa and gently pushed her down. "Now, what do you want?"

Lola glared up at him. He tried not to let the stubborn set of her mouth charm him, but it was difficult. There was something about her feisty temper that entertained him and always had. Not that he didn't have a healthy respect for her when she was angry—he absolutely did.

After several seconds she mumbled an obscenity, slumped against the cushions and said, "Chicken soup sounds good. I haven't been able to keep anything down, but suddenly I'm starving."

Erik began rummaging through the bags, pulling out the container he'd grabbed from Main Street Deli. With a pat on the hand as she'd passed it across the counter, Mrs. Houston, the owner, had promised him it would be just the thing to soothe Lola's tummy.

He didn't question how she knew what was wrong with Lola. There was little doubt the entire town was already aware of Lola's pregnancy and the circumstances leading to it.

Pulling open drawers until he found her spoons, Erik brought over both containers, along with a glass of ginger ale and a sleeve of crackers. He set the entire spread in front of her and pulled her coffee table closer. He ignored the way she glared at him for rearranging her furniture.

Erik sat beside her and started eating his soup. Mrs. Houston was right; it was pretty damn good.

He watched as Lola took a couple of tentative bites and then waited. Her entire body relaxed when she finally took a few more. The hum of satisfaction that rumbled through her chest echoed straight through his. The bliss that crossed her face was worth every damn penny and the multiple stops he'd made along the way.

They ate in silence. When she'd drained the bowl, Erik took it from her, brought everything to the kitchen and put the dishes into the dishwasher. Without a word, he refilled her glass, popped one of the movies he'd picked into her player and then settled back down beside her.

Lola stiffened. "I appreciate the soup more than you know, Erik. But it's time for you to leave." She tried to push up from the sofa, but his big hand across her thigh stalled her.

Erik felt the jolt of energy shoot up his arm. It shouldn't have surprised him. His body had always reacted that way to Lola, like she was a live wire. Flexing his fingers, he pulled his hand away.

"Relax. I'm only here to help, nothing more."

The way she looked at him cut straight through to his soul. The punch of turmoil and uncertainty she couldn't quite hide.

"We need to figure out how to be in the same room without all the tension and uncomfortable history churning between us. Consider this a first step. Let me stay for a little while. Make sure you're okay. For my peace of mind if nothing else. Please."

He watched her mouth soften, the tension that had tightened the edges of her eyes slipping away. Her shoulders rose and fell as she pulled in a deep breath and then let it out with a silent sigh.

"Okay."

She settled back against the sofa. At least she had a bit more color in her cheeks.

Lola was clearly trying to keep some distance between them, though. Erik couldn't help but look at the gap and feel the echo of it slam through him. He didn't want there to be any space. The last time he and Lola had watched a movie together, she'd been cuddled in his lap. In fact, they never actually finished watching that movie because neither of them could keep their hands off each other.

The memory rattled him. He didn't want to feel like this, like they were strangers when for so long he'd been closer to Lola than anyone.

And because he was perverse, about twenty minutes into the movie—a romantic comedy that he was paying zero attention to—Erik reached out and gently maneuvered Lola until she was leaning against him. Before she could voice a protest, he pressed his unfair advantage and began to massage his fingers across her scalp—her weakness, he knew from experience.

Her smothered moan zinged straight below his belt, but he ignored the reaction. That wasn't what this was about. They'd been friends long before they'd been lovers. He wanted that back—even if he probably shouldn't, or didn't deserve it.

Erik kept the motion up, enjoying the feel of her soft hair threading through his fingers. Her supple body melted slowly, trustingly against him. The smooth, even tempo of her breathing told him she'd drifted into sleep.

He stayed there, probably long after he should have left, because no part of him wanted to move. Six long years. A lot of experiences and emotions. Memories he fought against on a regular basis. And regrets. So many regrets. They all swirled in his head, somehow clouding things and leaving him restless and comfortable all at once.

It was late, closer to morning than night, when he finally scooped Lola into his arms and carried her to her bedroom at the back of the house. Tucking her beneath the covers, instinct made him press a kiss to her forehead like he had the right. The tight knot in his gut reminded him that he didn't.

Erik slowly moved through the house, checking that everything was secure. He turned off the TV and stood at her front door for several long seconds, a huge part of him wishing he could have stayed.

Leaving felt wrong.

6

LOLA HAD BEEN out of sorts all morning. Not entirely surprising for her lately, although today her disorientation had nothing to do with morning sickness and everything to do with the fact that she'd woken up with Erik's scent filling her lungs and a stupid smile curling her lips.

She was an idiot.

She couldn't seem to stop thinking about how sweet he'd been last night. Not that it really surprised her. He was always the kind of guy who took care of people. His need to protect and provide was an integral part of who he was.

She didn't have time for this. Or for morning sickness. It was a summer Saturday in Sweetheart and she had the Wilson-Billings wedding today. She and Misty Wilson had spent hours discussing what she wanted for her photographs. The bridal session had been beautiful and Misty had been amazing to work with. Not all brides were, so Lola appreciated when an easygoing one dropped into her lap.

The few times she'd met with the couple, it had been clear Misty and Sam were deeply in love, which just made her job so much easier and more enjoyable. She'd seen plenty of weddings over the years that she'd known would lead to marriages doomed to failure. Pictures never lied, and she'd often caught unguarded moments that told the true story, not necessarily the one people wanted to believe. Those moments made her job difficult.

But today, she was excited. There was just something about capturing the happiness of a new couple that always caused her own heart to flutter. She'd been looking forward to this job for weeks.

Lola dressed carefully, as she always did for weddings. Appropriate for the occasion, but not flashy enough to draw attention. It was a fine line, especially considering the equipment she'd be using stuck out enough. Misty wanted a candid feel to her photographs, capturing the real moments instead of the standard staged ones. This was Lola's specialty.

Strolling into the studio early, she checked her equipment, something she normally would have done the day before a big booking like this. Colt had done as much as he could, gathering the things she'd need. But it was her responsibility to make sure the equipment worked and she had everything once she left the studio.

She was in the middle of doing just that when the bell over the front door tinkled out a greeting. Damn, she'd forgotten to lock it behind her.

Already forming an apology, Lola rushed to the front. She'd ask whoever had come in to call Colt on

Monday to schedule an appointment. But the words froze on her lips when she breezed into the room to find Erik standing in the middle of her studio.

Her first thought was that the man was big, making the shabby-chic decor she'd so carefully assembled appear dainty and breakable simply by his presence. He was handsome, as always, and the impact of him stole her breath.

But what startled her more was the way he was dressed. As long as she'd known him, Erik had been a jeans and T-shirt kinda guy. When he was working, he wore his uniform and looked damn good in it. But she could probably count on one hand the number of times she'd seen him in a suit.

That was what he was wearing. Charcoal gray with a faint pinstripe, hands stuffed into the pockets of his pants. A crisp white shirt and a pewter tie that almost exactly matched his eyes. The material clung to his broad shoulders and tight thighs, somehow accentuating his strong body even while covering it up. It wasn't fair.

"What are you doing?" Lola blurted out.

"Colt mentioned this job was going to be a long one. I thought I'd come help."

"Dressed like that?"

Unease flashed through Erik's eyes as he glanced down the length of his own body. "What's wrong with what I'm wearing? Colt said you always dress to blend in with the guests at the wedding. You can't stand there and tell me this is inappropriate for a wedding."

No, no it wasn't. It was perfect. He was perfect. "I

try not to stand out. Take focus away from the bride and groom."

He shrugged. "Okay."

"Erik, every woman in the damn place is going to be staring at you. You know you're gorgeous and now you're walking, talking suit porn."

A strangled sound, a cross between a laugh and a wheeze, gurgled through his throat. "Excuse me?"

"Suit porn. Guys might like to look at half-naked women, but women like to look at well-dressed men. Trust me." Lola couldn't stop her gaze from slipping slowly down Erik's body and back up again. She was only human. "Right now, you're suit porn in the flesh."

Erik shifted on his feet. Wait. "Are you blushing?" she asked. That wasn't possible. She couldn't remember anything ever embarrassing Erik to the point of blushing.

"No. Maybe." His gaze narrowed. "Is that why you like going to these things so much? You get to stare at guys in suits?"

"No. I go to *these things* because it's my job and I love what I do. There's nothing quite as uplifting and hopeful as a couple who glow with the reality of love. Makes me believe the fairy tales really can come true."

Even though theirs had fallen apart.

She didn't say the words, but they still somehow managed to echo through the room around them. Erik took a step toward her. Lola stepped backward.

Nope, she wasn't going there. Not today. Not while she was already on edge and vulnerable from last night, the scent of him still somehow managing to fill her lungs even though he was halfway across the room.

Holding up her hands, Lola said, "I appreciate the offer of help, but I'm fine. Go home."

"No."

"What?"

Erik's mouth thinned and he deliberately ignored her upheld hands, closing the gap between them even though it was obvious she didn't want him to. Part of her expected him to grasp her by the arms, haul her in close and kiss the hell of out her.

Probably because that was what her traitorous body wanted.

Instead, he brushed past her—lighting her up when his arm grazed her shoulder—and continued down the hall to the pile of equipment she'd been gathering.

She followed him because…what else was she supposed to do?

"This stuff ready to go?"

"Yes, but—"

She felt a mixture of horror and happiness when he reached down and started looping straps over his shoulders and tucking tripods under his arms.

"I assume we're taking your car?" he asked.

"Yes."

Loaded down like a pack mule, completely uncaring that he was putting wrinkles in that perfect suit, Erik turned to her. "Okay, but I'm driving. You can waste energy arguing with me about it or you can hand over the keys and rest on the drive. But fair warning, if you dig in on this one, I'm going to dig in later, because I have no doubt there's going to come a time when you need a little break and refuse to take it. I'm here to make you. Your choice."

Lola stared at him, a little dumbfounded, slightly annoyed and a lot turned on. What was wrong with her?

Her confusion was all his fault. He was being sweet and infuriatingly demanding all at the same time. She realized he was trying to take care of her, which was nice even if she didn't actually need him to do it.

And it was infuriating because there was a time in her life when she'd wanted that from him. But she was older and stronger now. Independent and capable. And she didn't want to let herself depend on him for anything only to have the rug pulled out from under her when she least expected it. Again.

He was right. She could put her foot down and refuse to let him come with her. She'd handled plenty of weddings by herself. But she couldn't deny that it would be nice to have help today. Especially as she stared at him weighted down with all her equipment. She would have had to make multiple trips to carry it all.

"You already know where I'm going, don't you? Colt told you about my job today."

Lola's heart stuttered as a blazing smile stretched across his lips and dawned, bright and beautiful, in his deep gray eyes.

"Maybe." The single word left her wiggle room, but the glee in his gaze told her the real answer was yes. Damn her brother.

"I'm seriously going to hurt him."

"Yeah, right. We both know you'll bluster at him and do nothing."

With a sigh, Lola shook her head. "Whatever. But this is my job, Erik. I don't need you mucking around in it. When I say something, I need you to listen to me and do what I ask."

"Done." The fact that the word rushed past his lips did not give her confidence. Oh, she thought he really meant it, but at some point today they were going to clash.

And if she wasn't careful, that charged encounter would probably end with her back against a wall and his hard mouth claiming hers. Because that was how they'd always solved their arguments in the past. And old habits apparently died seriously hard.

ERIK HUNG IN the background, watching Lola work her magic. He'd hovered close, trying to anticipate what she might need so that he could provide it before she asked. Which was damn difficult considering he really didn't know what he was doing.

But it wasn't like this was the first time he'd watched Lola take photographs. Growing up, he could hardly remember a time when she didn't have a camera in her hand. First the old film one, then *his*. And each time she reached for the one he'd given her, he'd gotten a thrill of possessive pride.

Her obsession and talent had always intrigued him. He didn't have an artistic bone in his body. Physical labor, working with his hands, taking risks and powering through difficult situations with a body he'd fine-tuned to be strong, that he understood. He recognized beauty when he saw it, had witnessed it time and again in Lola's work. But while she had a talent for recognizing potential and capturing the perfect moment, he couldn't see it until her photographs framed it out for him. Her perception was both amazing and a little unsettling.

Lola easily rode herd over the chaotic wedding party, all without making it appear as though she was actually controlling anything. She confidently directed people here and there, from ninety-two-year-old grandma Wilson all the way down to an adorable toddler who had a death grip on a basket of rose petals and a wild-eyed expression that suggested she was going to lose it at any moment.

He'd never seen her shoot a wedding so had no idea her job was more cunning mastermind than artist sometimes. She interacted, soothed, bolstered confidence to get a smile. Somehow she managed to pull the best out of everyone.

Including him. She'd always seen the potential in him, which had been daunting and put more pressure on him to live up to her expectations than he'd realized…until he'd screwed up so badly.

What bothered him now was that Lola had been on her feet for almost six hours with pretty much no break. The minute they'd gotten there she'd jumped into action, bouncing between the room where the bride and her party were getting ready and the room where the groom and his men were preparing.

She captured breathtaking shots of the empty sanctuary decorated with fragrant flowers and stripes of late afternoon sunlight, showing him a few of the preliminary pictures. Somehow she managed to place herself at the perfect unobtrusive location to get candid shots through the ceremony. And now, at the reception, everyone else was enjoying the party. Lola was working.

At the moment she was crouched down getting a shot between the flower girl—who'd finally relinquished her basket—and Misty Wilson's nephew. The little girl had thrown her arms around the boy and was forcing him to dance with her like the adults. It was clear from the expression on the boy's face that he wanted nothing to do with the girl or the dancing.

Darkness had fallen outside, and through the wall of windows at the far end of the room, he could just make out a balcony with candlelit tables underneath the stars. Several people were enjoying the view over the expansive golf course at the Marin Country Club, but the balcony was quieter and less crowded than the ballroom.

Exactly what he needed.

Because wisdom had come with age, Erik formulated a plan to get Lola to take the break he knew she needed but was unlikely to allow. In his younger years he probably would have simply marched her across the room to an empty table. His lips twitched at the thought. She'd have given him shit the whole way, but she would have gone because he would have been whispering naughty things into her ear until she forgot what she was upset about. Then she'd melt against him in that way that drove him mad and made his chest swell.

He was no longer certain Lola would follow him anywhere. So it was a good thing he'd gotten smarter.

Trailing a line of people through the buffet, Erik loaded down a plate with food and grabbed two forks. He crossed to the balcony— the night air was warm, heavy with the scent of flowers from the garden below. A breeze had kicked up, making the summer evening perfect for being outside. He picked a table in a secluded corner. Darkness, shadows and a low brick wall would shield them from everyone else. He plopped the plate onto the table.

He went back in and found her taking photographs of the new bride as she bent down to wrap her arms around her great-grandmother. Erik drifted close to Lola, waiting. After several minutes, she grumbled, "Stop hovering."

"I'm not hovering."

"You are. I can feel you back there, hovering. I'll take a break in a bit."

Yeah, right. They both knew that was a lie.

Slipping up behind her, Erik wrapped an arm around her waist and pressed his mouth to her ear. The spicy citrus scent of her swirled around him, making him light-headed as every blood cell in his body immediately rushed below his belt. It was hard to think with his lips pressed to her skin and her body snuggled against his. Nope, not the time or the place.

"You remember what I said earlier? I'm changing the deal. You may have let me drive, but after hours on your feet you need a break."

She started to open her mouth to protest, but Erik didn't let her get the words out.

"Now or I'll take all your equipment to the car. Your choice."

Lola's head whipped around. Her body stiffened as she glared at him. "You're being an asshole."

"Maybe, but that's what you need. You haven't stopped moving for the last six hours, Lola. You need to eat something before you collapse. If you won't take care of yourself, then I'm here to do the job for you."

Her glare intensified, but that didn't sway him.

"I've been taking care of myself for a very long time, Erik McKnight. I don't need you."

Her words were like a punch in the gut. Because they were true. And that hurt like hell.

Erik shook it off, focusing on her. "Be smart. I've got a plate for you. Just sit down for a few and refuel. Then you can go back to doing what you love."

She hesitated before finally giving him a sharp nod. Running his hand down her arm, he tried to ignore the smoldering embers that crackled along his palm. He twined his fingers with hers and then led her through the maze of tables to where he'd left the food.

Lola gently placed her camera on the table—within quick reach—before settling into the chair he pulled out for her. Erik sank down beside her and nudged the plate in her direction. The wind teased at the ends of her hair, stirring them in a way that reminded him just how soft it was. He longed to bury his fingers deep inside and hold her head still as he devoured her mouth.

Shadows and flickering light from the candle between them played across her golden skin. She was gorgeous, always, but even more so right then. His fingers itched to reach out and trail over her cheek and jaw, tip up her chin so he could lean in and taste her lips.

Oblivious to his train of thought, Lola picked up the fork, letting it drift over the pile of options for several seconds before diving in for a bite of thinly sliced roast beef. Glancing up, she asked, "You're not eating?"

Picking up the second fork, Erik slowly stabbed a mushroom stuffed with cheese and herbs, popping it into his mouth. "Easier if we just share. You probably won't finish all of this anyway, but I wasn't sure what you'd want, so I grabbed a little of everything."

"So I see." She slid the plate in his direction and chose a bite of au gratin potatoes for herself. Without saying anything, Lola used her fork to slide all of the mushrooms over to his side of the plate.

Because she knew he loved them?

There was a time when a moment like this with Lola would have been easy and comfortable. Not right now. The air crackled with energy. Erik could feel it, raising the hairs on the back of his neck and tightening every muscle in his body.

Everyone else at the wedding had spent all day watching the bride and groom. He, on the other hand, had spent all day watching Lola, sending him into this hyperaware state that had been building inside him for hours.

He was dangerously on edge, everything inside him throbbing with the need for more of her. He realized she wouldn't welcome anything from him, but he couldn't squash his body's reaction.

Which only got worse when Lola's thigh brushed against his.

He couldn't be this close to her and not want to touch her. Some instinct was urging him on, beating out a tattoo in his brain that was getting harder and harder to ignore. It wasn't helping that someone had placed little bells around the reception room, and every time someone rang one, the bride and groom had to kiss.

That only made his mind return to the sinful taste of Lola's mouth. Each soft tinkle was torture, ramping up the need inside him to a fever pitch.

It all came to a head when Lola pushed away the half-finished plate. She stood, her chair scraping against the stone beneath their feet. The heel on her shoe caught in a crack and she stumbled. Her arms windmilled and her body swayed.

Erik reached for her without thought, snagging her before she could lose her balance and go down. He pushed her deeper into the corner of the alcove, settling her back against the dark red brick of the building for support.

And it was all too much.

His body was flush against hers. Breasts and hips crushed to him in a way that had instant sparks lighting up his entire body. His thighs bracketed one of hers, the heat of her seeping through his pants.

But it was her expression that really did him in.

Lola stared up at him, a combination of heat and surprise filling those deep brown eyes. Her lips were parted on a silent *oh* that morphed as her tongue shot out to swipe across her plump pink lips.

With a groan, Erik bent down and snagged her mouth. The kiss was far from soft. It was an avalanche of everything he'd been bottling up. It was heat and need and flamed hot and hard.

Lola made a sound, a mingled whimper and groan. Her hands found his waist and hovered, neither holding him in place nor pushing him away.

The taste of her was madness, and it wasn't nearly enough. Erik leaned into her more. His palms, planted on the brick at either side of her head, flexed. He wanted to grab her, but at least a tiny part of his brain must have been working, because he hesitated.

Erik wasn't sure how long it lasted. Enough to leave them both winded. Lola finally pushed him back several inches.

"No," she whispered. "No."

She scooted out from under his body, putting even more space between them. His chest ached from breathing too hard and something else he didn't want to think about right now.

Slowly he turned, straightened, forced his balled fists into his pockets so he wouldn't reach for her again.

Lola stared at him, framed by the windows at her back. The party raged behind her, everyone laughing, dancing, happy. The groom twirled the bride across the floor, her face tilted back with delight and bright with wonder.

While Lola stared up at him, misery and panic stamped across every feature.

Shaking her head, she said, "I will not do this with you again, Erik. I can't."

He watched her leave, frozen as if he'd been cemented to the spot. Everything inside him throbbed, with agony and need.

But she was right.

That kiss hadn't been fair to either of them.

The problem was, they were going to have to figure out how to deal with each other without letting the past become a specter fueled by hate or this physical need driving them to sabotage the rest of their lives.

But tomorrow was soon enough to figure out how to move forward. Erik pulled out the chair Lola had used and sprawled into the shadows. For right now, he'd stay where he was. Because he didn't trust himself not to put his hands all over her again.

7

LOLA GROANED AS she rolled out of bed. Sunday was her day. She tried not to go into the studio, not even for editing or paperwork. Especially after a long shoot like the one last night.

Thoughts of the wedding immediately turned to thoughts of that kiss. Which immediately sent liquid warmth spilling through her veins. She'd always known Erik could kiss, but…damn.

She'd been hyperaware of him all night, even before the kiss. Standing beside her, anticipating her needs, taking care of her…at least until the end when he'd kept his distance. She should have been grateful for the reprieve, but she wasn't.

His attention had been sweet and unsettling all at the same time. He'd made her edgy. Several times she'd bitten back the need to tell him to give her room to breathe—doing that would have been admitting he was affecting her. And she refused to do that.

So instead, she'd gotten a little too close to the fire

last night and felt it singe her. No more. She was proud of herself for pushing him away, because it had been touch and go there for a few moments. Everything inside her was begging just to give in and take what she wanted.

But she knew there was potential for a hell of a lot more if she let herself get wrapped up in him again. Nope, the smarter choice was to draw a clear line and refuse to step over it.

That was exactly what she'd done for the rest of the evening, and Erik had been quiet when he'd dropped her off at the studio. He hadn't even insisted on following her home—not that she'd wanted him to, but she was surprised he hadn't offered.

Lola shuffled out to the kitchen, stared longingly at her coffeepot, and then popped in a pod of decaffeinated tea instead. Her head was muzzy as she waited for it to brew.

It was just after ten, way past her normal time to get up. But Lola was cutting herself some slack today. Her plans involved a close relationship with her pjs, her bed and a book she'd been dying to read.

All of that got blown out of the water when a loud knock sounded on her front door. The last person she expected to find standing on her porch was Erik. Holding a picnic basket.

"What are you doing?" The door was open and the words out of her mouth before she'd meant to say them. If she'd been a little less groggy, she would have simply ignored the knock and pretended not to be home.

Without waiting for an invitation—that was really

starting to piss her off—Erik slipped inside. He set the basket down on her kitchen counter.

"We're going to the lake. I know the studio is closed today and you have the day off." He held up his hands to forestall her protest. "We need to talk, Lola. In a relaxing public setting that won't lead to arguments—" something enigmatic crossed his expression "—or kisses. We have some important things to figure out and not a lot of time."

She didn't need the reminder that soon he'd be leaving for California.

"You can't have a bad day at the lake. It's summer. Come on."

A lazy day at the lake did sound nice. She hadn't taken the time since the girls had dragged her out there at the end of last season.

Grumbling, Lola finally said, "Fine. But no funny business."

A smirk crossed his face. "Remember who you're talking to."

Which didn't do anything to settle her nerves.

"Scoot. Go get ready. We're wasting daylight."

And all the good spots would be taken if they didn't hurry.

Disappearing into her bedroom, Lola was careful to shut and lock the door. Not that she expected Erik to barge in where he wasn't wanted. The lock was more for herself than for him.

Ten minutes later, Lola stared at herself in the mirror and bit back a groan. She'd never been the kind of woman to care overly much about the slight curve of her stomach—and the black bikini she'd bought just after Memorial Day on a shopping trip with the girls looked just fine. For now.

What bothered her was the thought of spending the day with Erik while she was practically naked. Just the thought of Erik's eyes on her had her body tingling with anticipation.

Maybe she'd just keep her cover-up on all day. She buttoned up the oversized men's shirt she used and didn't bother putting anything else on since it hung almost to her knees. Tossing a towel, sunscreen, straw cowgirl hat and the book she'd planned to read today into her bag, Lola headed back down the hallway, purposely avoiding a second glance in the full-length mirror.

She did not care how she looked. She'd tied her hair in a messy knot on the top of her head and smoothed some tinted moisturizer with sunscreen across her face. How she looked didn't matter. She wouldn't let it matter.

At the last second, she grabbed her camera, the one she kept at home and used for her personal pictures—the one Erik had given her—and added it to the pile.

Erik reached for her stuff. Lola reluctantly relinquished her tote but kept hold of the camera in its bag. It didn't escape her notice that his gaze snagged on the worn fabric. It was as familiar to him as it was to her, and a tiny flutter of panic ghosted through her belly.

She followed him outside and waited as he stowed her things behind the driver's seat before sliding into his truck. She immediately noticed the two steaming cups sitting in the console. The heavenly scent of coffee wafted up to her and she groaned.

"I'd kill for some coffee right about now."

"No need for that. Yours is right there."

She frowned at him. "I can't have coffee."

"No, you can't have caffeine. Yours is decaf."

Slumping down in her seat, Lola crossed her arms over her chest. Yes, she realized she was pouting, and right now she didn't care. "That's just cruel, Erik. Decaf isn't even worth the effort."

He shrugged. "Seven months is a long time, Lo. You might want to at least try your options before deciding they suck."

The longer she sat in the truck, surrounded by that mouth-watering scent, the more she thought maybe he was right. Finally, unable to resist, Lola reached for the cup and cradled it in her hands before taking a sip.

And nearly orgasmed at the burst of flavor across her tongue. It had been a long week since she'd found out she was pregnant. "Are you sure this is decaf?"

"Absolutely."

Okay, so maybe the next few months wouldn't be so bad if she could still have this pleasure.

Erik chatted as they drove, filling the twenty-minute ride with inane comments about people he'd run into and things he'd done in the last six years. By the time they arrived, she was laughing at some story he'd told, comfortable enough with him to reach over and smack his arm.

That was one of Erik's many talents. Somehow he'd always had the ability to put people at ease, no matter

FREE Merchandise 'in the Cards for you!

Dear Reader,

We're giving away FREE MERCHANDISE!

Seriously, we'd like to reward you for reading this novel by giving you **FREE MERCHANDISE** worth over $20 retail. And no purchase is necessary!

You see the Jack of Hearts sticker above? Paste that sticker in the box on the Free Merchandise Voucher inside. Return the Voucher today... and we'll send you Free Merchandise!

Thanks again for reading one of our novels—and enjoy your Free Merchandise with our compliments!

Pam Powers

Pam Powers

P.S. Look inside to see what Free Merchandise is **"in the cards"** for you!

FREE MERCHANDISE VOUCHER

2 FREE BOOKS and **2 FREE GIFTS**

Please send my Free Merchandise, consisting of
2 Free Books and **2 Free Mystery Gifts**.
I understand that I am under no obligation to buy
anything, as explained on the back of this card.

225/326 HDL GLTD

Please Print

FIRST NAME

LAST NAME

ADDRESS

APT.#   CITY

STATE/PROV.   ZIP/POSTAL CODE

NO PURCHASE NECESSARY!

HD-517-FM17

▼ If offer card is missing write to: Reader Service, P.O. Box 1341, Buffalo, NY 14240-8531 or visit www.ReaderService.com ▼

BUSINESS REPLY MAIL
FIRST-CLASS MAIL   PERMIT NO. 717   BUFFALO, NY

POSTAGE WILL BE PAID BY ADDRESSEE

READER SERVICE
PO BOX 1341
BUFFALO NY 14240-8571

NO POSTAGE
NECESSARY
IF MAILED
IN THE
UNITED STATES

the situation. His charm and self-possession just translated to others. It was a skill she'd often envied.

Lake Wetumpka stretched through three counties and was a hot spot for summer activity. Lots of little coves had been carved from the forest surrounding the huge lake. The resort Lexi's husband, Blake, had built several years ago stood on the opposite bank from where Erik had parked, breathtaking even as it blended into the natural backdrop in the distance.

Lola could see clusters of guests as they took advantage of the water sports the resort offered. While it looked fun, her body wasn't quite up for that kind of activity today. She had something a little less strenuous in mind, so she didn't object when Erik grabbed her hand and led her down a path through the thick trees. They arrived at a quiet clearing. The ground was brown and sandy, a mixture of dirt, moss and large grains of sand. Instead of the shells found on the coast not far away, smooth stones were scattered about by the lake.

This was where they'd always come. Not just the large group of friends who managed to gather on hot summer days, but she and Erik alone.

The memory of one particular night was scored into her brain. This was where she'd lost her virginity. Had Erik chosen this spot because it was where they'd always come, or because of those particular memories?

Erik shooed her away when she tried to help him set up their stuff. Unlike when they were younger and all they needed was a towel, today he'd brought an armload of paraphernalia. A picnic basket with drinks and food. A couple of low-slung beach chairs and even an umbrella that he insisted on setting up so the shade fell over her.

She didn't have the heart to tell him she didn't need all the fussing. Not after he spent fifteen minutes making their spot perfect.

The heat derailed her plan to keep her shirt on for the entire day, sweat pearling on her skin already. Comfort won out over worry, and she dropped her shirt onto the ground before heading for the water.

Wading in, she dunked her head under the surface. The sensation of the cool water on her heated skin was amazing relief. Kicking onto her back, Lola began to float, letting the water cradle her. Her eyes shut against the glare of the sun.

She felt him as he moved close, her body reacting to his nearness like a metal filing to a magnet.

His fingers brushed against her body beneath the water, and she sucked in a breath. But the touch was fleeting, there and gone before she could really register it. She wanted more. Which was exactly why she rolled onto her belly and took a huge stroke to move away.

Filling the longing with something other than them, she said, "It's been so long since I've visited the lake."

"That's a shame. There's a lake back home, different but the same in a lot of ways. Some of the guys and I make a point of going out there a couple times during the summer when we're not out on calls."

"Your friends. Mostly other smoke jumpers?"

He shrugged, his gaze pulled away. "Mostly."

"Tell me about them." The request popped out of her mouth before she could even really think about it. The stories he'd shared on the car ride yesterday had piqued her interest. A huge part of her wanted him to fill in the blanks for her. Wanted to know all about the life he'd lived and the things he'd done without her.

The rest of her didn't want the reminder that he'd moved on, walked away and built something she had no part of.

He chuckled, and a wicked little grin twisted his mouth. "You know I've moved around a lot, so it's difficult to form lasting friendships when you're there and gone. But smoke jumping lends itself to camaraderie."

"Sure, putting your lives in each other's hands…you have to trust and respect the guy standing beside you."

"Exactly. I've been in Cali for a couple years now."

The longest he'd been anywhere, aside from Sweetheart. She almost asked him why he'd stayed there when he'd ditched everywhere else but was afraid the answer would be a woman, even if he wasn't seeing anyone now. She wasn't ready to hear details of his love life. Maybe never would be.

"I'm close to three or four of the guys. But it's different, you know?"

She did know. She knew how close he'd been with Colt and the other guys at the station. When you spent so much time together, especially under stressful situations, it was difficult not to become close. She'd watched those same bonds form between her dad and the men he served with, the guys who would come over to their house for summer barbecues and football games. She'd seen the anxieties shared by the women who lived with the same fear her mother had, and the kids who dealt with their dads missing dance recitals or Christmas mornings.

She'd been that kid. She'd become that woman when her brother and Erik had joined the department.

Then, when he'd left, he hadn't just walked away from her. He'd walked away from his best friend when Colt had needed him most.

She needed to remember that. He'd walked away before. Had continued the same thing as he traveled from place to place. But putting down roots in California... maybe he'd changed?

Not that it really mattered. Because even if he had, those roots weren't in Sweetheart.

"Look," she said, "I didn't mean to bring up things that don't matter anymore."

Something sharp flashed across Erik's face, and faster than she'd expected, his hands wrapped around her upper arms, holding her in place. The lake wasn't deep here, probably around four feet. Water sluiced down her body as he pulled her up to stand, drawing her in until his face was inches from hers.

Anger, anguish and something deeper twisted his mouth. "Don't tell me it doesn't matter, Lo. As long as Colt is in that chair, it'll matter."

She watched the turmoil rolling through him, felt the reverberation of it deep inside her own chest. For so long she'd wanted to blame him, make him the scapegoat, even as Colt told her she shouldn't. Even as her own conscience twinged when she tried. Now, staring into the truth of the pain he lived with every day...she couldn't do it anymore. Everything inside her wanted to make it go away. Wanted to soothe him, because she couldn't stand to see him ache.

Instinct and memory had her rising onto her toes until her mouth touched his. For a moment, a breath, before his grip on her arms tightened, pushing her away.

So many mixed signals. She couldn't process them, especially with her brain short-circuiting from the simple feel of his lips against hers.

She hated herself a little for leaning into the space he put between them, chasing more. When was she *really* going to learn to let him go?

"Don't," he growled. Pain flashed through her chest. Did he really not want her to touch him? But then he said, "Don't try to use what's between us as a bandage."

Lola sucked in a harsh breath. "What is between us, Erik? I don't really know anymore. Chemistry and fire, that kiss last night proved that. But that's always been there."

His fingers flexed, squeezing her arm in a way that made her body throb. She wanted him to touch so much more. Instead, he let her go, dropping his hands and leaving her skin cold without his warmth.

"I'm trying to be on my best behavior here, Lola. To do the right thing."

The right thing. She was so damn tired of fighting what Erik made her feel. Were they ever going to be in the same room together without striking sparks off each other? Maybe she just needed to let go, give in and let fate take control.

Maybe she needed closure, a moment that wasn't fueled with pain or guilt or alcohol.

"What exactly do you think is the right thing, Erik? Because I don't know anymore. What I do know is that being this close to you and not having the right to touch you makes me ache."

He closed his eyes, making her wonder whether he was praying or searching for strength.

But when he opened them again, she realized it didn't matter. The heat that engulfed her left her skin feeling too tight and ready to burst, spilling everything she was at his feet.

"You always have the right to touch me, Lo. Any time. Any way."

A part of her wished that was true—the part of her that couldn't say no to what he was offering, even as the rest of her screamed that she should. That nothing between them had actually been settled and she was simply kicking the can down the road, delaying the inevitable and setting herself up for more pain.

Reaching out, she pressed her hand against the hard planes of his chest. The heat of his skin burned straight through her. Cool droplets clung to him, sparkling in the sunlight. And she was done denying what she wanted.

Leaning forward, Lola ran her tongue across his skin, collecting the droplets and savoring the taste of him.

"Lola," he groaned deep in his throat. The rumble of her name rolling off his tongue pulled any last resistance out from under her.

This was what she wanted. He was what she wanted.

And she was strong enough to take what was in front of her. She'd worry about the aftermath later.

Erik gripped her arms, and for a moment Lola worried he was going to try to shove her away again. But he didn't. Instead, Erik wrapped an arm around her back and boosted her higher against him.

And there was no denying he was as turned on as she was. The hard length of his erection pressed into the open V of her thighs, making her want even more.

Their night together at the fire station had been good, but it had been almost a distant dream. Like many she'd had since Erik left. Hazy and liquid heat.

Right now, in broad daylight, with nothing between them but the burning desire they couldn't deny…this was reality and it felt amazing.

Erik's mouth found hers, kissing her and reclaiming what had always been his. Memories and need lapped against her just as surely as the water against her skin, eroding everything but the way Erik made her feel. Had always made her feel.

It was déjà vu and something new all wrapped together, and it made her head spin. His lips roamed down her throat and across her collarbones. Scooping her up, Erik carried her out of the lake, all without breaking his assault on her senses.

He grabbed their towels and tossed them onto the sandy ground before dropping to his knees and stretching her out.

For several seconds he stared at her. Long enough that Lola had to fight the urge to squirm. She'd never been the kind of woman to care what others thought of her, but Erik's opinion had always mattered, even when she hadn't wanted it to.

She wasn't the same girl she'd been six years ago. The expression in Erik's eyes seemed to mean he didn't care that she'd changed. Heat and intensity scraped across her skin as his smoky eyes moved slowly down her entire body. She felt the touch of his gaze like a caress. Goose bumps pebbled her skin, and she fought down a tremble.

"Cold?" he asked, his voice rough and deep.

"No," she whispered.

His lips quirked up into a knowing grin that immediately changed the entire dynamic of the moment into something more familiar and comfortable. Reaching up, she smacked his shoulder. "Cocky bastard."

His grin only widened. And any last nerves she'd had fled. This was the playful, brash boy she'd known her entire life beneath the layer of the strong stranger he'd become. For the moment, she had her Erik back, and she was going to enjoy it while she could.

As if sensing the change in her mood, Erik latched his mouth onto the side of her neck and sucked. Lola groaned—he knew that was a weakness of hers—and then bucked when he kept going. "If you leave a mark I have to explain…"

Against her skin, he chuckled. "Wasn't I always careful?"

"Mmm, most of the time." But not always. She'd had to wear scarves or turtleneck sweaters to hide his enthusiasm from her dad on more than one occasion.

Back then she'd been avoiding a confrontation, protecting him just as much as herself. Now she wasn't ready or willing to explain.

His mouth roamed over her shoulder, down her ribs and across her tummy. He nipped and sucked. Licked and ghosted with his lips. And her body slowly, thoroughly burned. Lola had no idea how long he tortured her—could have been five minutes, could have been five hours. Either way, she was panting and delirious.

Never in her life had she wished for a smaller bathing suit, but now she did, since that seemed to be the barrier he wouldn't cross.

"Erik, touch me," she finally whispered.

"Isn't that what I'm doing?"

She whimpered, pressing her hips up to rub against the hard plane of his thigh. "No, I'm pretty sure you're not. Not where I want."

That wicked grin was back when he pulled away and stared down at her. "And where do you want?"

Pushing up onto her elbows, Lola grasped the knot at the back of her neck and yanked, doing the same to the one behind her back until the bikini top she wore fell into her lap. Cupping her breasts, she pulled in a mixed gasp of pleasure and pain, so sensitive from her pregnancy. "Here."

Erik's gaze sharpened on her breasts. He reached for one, rolling the distended nipple between thumb and forefinger, drawing a groan from deep inside her.

"Yes, there. More."

Leaning forward, Erik slid his tongue across the other, a soft, barely there caress, all the while never letting up on the pressure with his fingers. The combination of hard and soft nearly had her mind exploding.

"Tell me if this hurts," he murmured against her skin. Always looking out of her. Always protecting.

"It doesn't hurt, exactly. My breasts are just achy lately. But that feels so damn good," she said, threading her fingers through his hair and holding him right there.

She wanted more. Everything. And unwilling to wait any longer, Lola wrapped her legs around Erik's, pushed up with her hips and flipped them both.

It might have been funny, the way he blinked up at her, disoriented, from the ground. But she was too pre-occupied for that.

Stretching out over him, Lola found his mouth and sucked on his bottom lip. She straddled his hips, the V between her thighs perfectly cradling his hard erection. The feel of him was unbelievable and exactly what she needed.

Rolling her hips, Lola relished the hiss she pulled from him.

"Lola." Her name was a warning she fully intended to ignore.

"Erik," she countered, lifting up onto her knees and working her bikini bottoms off.

They were alone for now, protected in the little alcove by the curve of land and huge stand of trees surrounding them. Anyone could ride up from the other side of the lake, but Lola didn't care. The danger added a forbidden spice, not that sex with Erik wasn't already dangerous enough.

Her risk was rewarded when Erik's big hands coasted down her body and across her skin. The heat of him blazed through her. The feel so familiar and right.

He parted the folds of her sex and groaned when he found her dripping wet. "How am I supposed to say no to this?"

"You aren't."

Lifting his hips, Erik pushed at the waistband of his trunks until she took pity on them both and helped him take them off.

God, he was gorgeous. Tanned skin, miles of muscles that he'd achieved through the strenuous requirements of his job. All across his hip and thigh were tiny white puckers of flesh, scars he didn't have six years ago. Reminders she didn't really want right now about the dangers of his job.

But she couldn't ignore them, either.

Leaning down, she placed kiss after kiss across each one, losing count at twenty-five. Tears stung the backs of her eyes, thinking about him in danger. In pain. Suffering alone.

"Lola." This time her name was a prayer and an apology that he didn't owe her, at least not for this.

She shook her head, continuing to do exactly what she wanted, offering him solace even if it was too late. Silently accepting, him, the life he'd led without her.

His fingers in her hair, Erik gently brought her gaze back to his. The light and heat there singed her all over again, sending a rush of need barreling through her.

"Grab my wallet from the bag, okay?"

Without question, Lola tipped back onto one arm and rummaged around until she returned triumphantly with his wallet. Erik didn't make the task easy. He took the opportunity of her body stretched out to run his fingers along her torso and across her parted thighs.

She nearly collapsed when he buried two fingers deep inside her sex, pulling a strangled cry from her throat. His thumb found her clit and she saw stars. Lola was left panting, hips gyrating for relief.

But that wasn't what she wanted at all.

Pushing back up, she gripped Erik's wrist and stopped the motion of his fingers deep inside her.

He looked up at her quizzically. "I want to feel you inside me," she said, "and if you keep doing that I'm going to come in no time flat."

"Baby, I don't care how you come. As far as I'm concerned, watching you break apart is one of the wonders of the world."

"Just what every woman wants to hear." Tossing his wallet onto his chest, she waggled a finger at it. "Condom. Maybe this one won't break. I assume that's what you were looking for, not your license to prove you're over eighteen and not jailbait?"

Beneath her, Erik's entire body shook with suppressed laughter. "How can you make me laugh at the same time I have my fingers buried between your thighs?"

"Talent. Chop-chop, lover boy."

This time, it was Lola's turn for a little torture. Erik needed both hands to flip through his wallet, hunting that precious little packet, and she was never one to miss an opportunity.

Placing her hands on his chest, Lola spread her legs wide and perfectly positioned the wet heat of her sex along the hard ridge of his erection. She rolled her hips, sliding up and down.

"Witch," he groaned, even as his entire body twitched beneath her. Over and over, she rocked her hips. Lost in the sensation they both created, she didn't even notice Erik had found what he was looking for until she was suddenly on her back again.

The wind was knocked out of her, not by the force of impact, but by the sudden change in location and space.

He growled, latched on to her neck and sucked hard. She laughed, a wicked sound she rather liked, one she hadn't heard from herself in a very long time.

Rocking back onto his knees, Lola watched him roll the condom down the length of his erection before positioning the head at the entrance to her body. He paused, watching her for several seconds. It took her a few to realize he was waiting for permission. "Yes. Please. Now."

With one deep thrust, Erik slid inside. Her body didn't resist him. It never had. She simply melted around him, giving and taking everything.

Beneath the massive strength and force of his body, Lola felt pinned to the earth. Anchored in a way she hadn't experienced for years, and hadn't realized she'd missed so much.

And that was before he'd even started to move. In and out, slow and steady. Torturous and unbelievably amazing. The push and pull of their bodies was like a perfectly composed photograph—light and shape working together to form beauty.

Lola's hips moved with him, searching for even one more shred of connection between them. Her entire body tightened, quaking on the need to let go. But she kept holding on, wanting more, afraid to let the experience end.

The feel of him against her was too good. Too right.

But bringing his mouth to her ear, Erik whispered, "Let go." And she couldn't stop herself from falling over the edge.

His name tore from her lips as her entire body trembled. The orgasm shattered her, everything else in the world blacking out and condensing to nothing more than Erik's glorious body inside her, surrounding her.

It wasn't long before he joined her, his own grunts morphing into the sound of her name, a panted benediction forced through parted lips.

Together they collapsed onto the ground, a tangle of arms and legs that she wasn't sure she'd ever have the strength to unravel.

His hand ghosted down her back, across her shoulders and over one thigh. "Are you all right?"

"Mmm," was as close to a word as she could muster.

He chuckled, rolled and tucked her into the warm shelter of his body.

She was languid and spent. So tired and yet somehow so alive.

"Don't let me fall asleep in the sun," she said. "The last thing I need is to burn."

Reaching over them, Erik adjusted the umbrella so it covered them.

"Sleep, baby. I've got you."

8

THE NAP DID nothing but make Lola more tired. No matter what, she couldn't seem to get enough sleep. And as much as she'd loved it, the time in the sun—and the romp with Erik—hadn't helped. The rest of the day she just felt groggy.

It was early evening by the time they drove up to her front door and Erik unloaded the car.

Nerves fluttered in her belly whenever he brushed close. Their afternoon together should have mellowed her out. Instead, it only seemed to make her cravings more intense.

Which was no doubt the problem.

She half expected Erik to drop her stuff inside the front door and disappear. She should have known better. Instead, he took the picnic basket to her kitchen and started unpacking. And then vanished down her hallway with the bag of towels.

Lola nearly melted when she heard the distinct sound of the washer coming on. He was doing her laundry. How was she supposed to stay strong in the face of all this? He rocked her world, took care of her because he wanted to and, without being asked, did household chores.

She was pretty sure the crack she heard was the hard shell she'd formed around her heart when he walked away. It was disintegrating into tiny pieces.

Crap.

Because even though on paper Erik sounded like a great guy—and he was—there was still the little problem that he was going to leave her. Again.

His life was in California, along with his reckless, dangerous job that had him parachuting out of planes to fight out-of-control fires. She'd lost her mother. Spent years worrying about losing her father. And watched as her brother lay helpless in a hospital bed, discovering he'd never walk again.

Not to mention, Erik had a nasty habit of leaving when things got tough.

She could not count on him. Period.

But, God, at the moment it was hard to remember all the reasons she should keep her distance. Erik was the man she'd loved for so long. The man she'd expected to spend the rest of her life with. And now he was the father of her baby.

So what was she supposed to do now? Go to the bedroom, strip naked and wait for round two? That idea held so much appeal she had to squeeze her thighs together to stave off the spike of desire.

Or maybe she should cook dinner. Yep, that was what she was going to do. He'd fed her lunch and taken her out for a relaxing day. She would return the favor.

She was leaning into the fridge, rummaging around, trying to decide what to cook, when he set a hand on her back, startling her. Lola let out a yelp as her head hit the top shelf of the fridge.

Hands on her hips, Erik pulled her backward and out. "Are you okay?"

"No."

With a frown, he found the spot on her head and rubbed. "I'm sorry."

That wasn't where she ached. The minute he touched her—anywhere—her body went up in flames. It was frustrating and exhilarating, his physical effect on her.

Squeezing her eyes shut, Lola took a deep breath and tried to find her center of gravity. She was not the kind of woman to lose her head over a guy.

Especially a guy who had burned her once already.

"It's fine. You startled me," she said, extricating herself from his hold, where it was all too tempting to stay. "Thought I'd make us some dinner. Nothing fancy. Tomato soup and grilled cheese?"

"Comfort food at its finest. But I can make it. Why don't you sit down?"

Because they'd had this argument several times already, Lola decided to take a different tack and completely ignore his question. She pulled out the ingredients she needed, placed a skillet on the burner to warm and then dumped a can of soup into a saucepan to heat.

If she sat still it wasn't going to be good. She needed to *do something* otherwise her libido and her brain were going to war. Besides, she could not let herself get used to having Erik pamper her. He was going home soon, and she'd be here alone.

Which was fine. Really, it was. She'd simply ignore that pesky ache in the center of her chest.

She concentrated on the mundane tasks in front of her, throwing some spices into the soup just as her mom had taught her. Within fifteen minutes, Lola had dinner plated. They were both sitting on the bar stools at her kitchen counter, blowing on the first mouthwatering spoonfuls of soup.

It tasted so good. Like warmth and home. One of the best memories she had of her mother was laughing and sharing a bowl of tomato soup. She couldn't remember how old she was the first time they'd had Lola/Mommy time—maybe four or five. It didn't matter. The taste of it and the memories always made her smile.

Just as the camaraderie and easiness that always came with Erik made her comfortable. They joked and teased. Poked fun at each other and reminisced. And each time he touched her felt like lightning striking her skin.

Together they cleaned up the kitchen, and Lola allowed herself a sigh of relief. Surely he'd go home now, and her body could release all this pent-up tension.

But the minute she flipped the light off above the sink, his hands settled on the soft curve of her hips, and it became crystal clear he had no intention of letting her off that easily.

ERIK HAD SENSED Lola's nervous energy from the minute they'd walked in her front door. He'd been in her house on more than one occasion lately without causing that kind of reaction.

But the lake had changed everything.

Even if neither of them was quite ready to deal with how.

They hadn't talked about what being together meant. And it was clear Lola wasn't ready to have that conversation. Instead, he thought of another way—a less complicated way that they'd always managed to get right even when everything else was going wrong—that would work in the meantime.

Erik had no intention of letting Lola's nerves or her overactive brain take away this potential relationship before they'd even had a chance to explore what could be. He knew if he did what she wanted and left her alone tonight, by the morning she'd have her walls back up, refusing to entertain the possibility of a second chance to get this right.

He'd never claimed to be honorable and had no problems pressing whatever advantage he had. So maybe he'd intentionally touched her all through dinner, not just because it gave him pleasure but because he enjoyed the way her body reacted to his simplest caresses.

The lightest stroke of his hand against her thigh caused goose bumps to trail up her leg. The scrape of his arm against her shoulder sent a shiver through her body. And leaning close, letting the warmth of his breath brush across her neck, drew her nipples into tight knots that made his mouth water for another taste.

She could deny it all she wanted, but her body couldn't lie.

Now that any possible barrier she could put between

them had been taken care of, Erik had every intention of proving to her that he was right. Even though she had no idea they'd spent the last couple of hours silently arguing.

The minute she flipped off the light, Erik moved closer. She turned and he was right there, his tall body looming over hers in the muted darkness that surrounded them. Bracketing her hips, he pinned her against the island counter, giving her no place to run.

She licked her lips, drawing her gaze slowly up his body until her deep brown eyes bored into his. "What are you doing?" she asked. She didn't whisper or quiver or play coy. She met him head-on. And that was one of the many things he loved about this woman.

Her confidence and backbone were sexy as hell.

"Let me ask you something, Lola."

Her eyes narrowed and her mouth thinned, but the tiny pulse in the center of her throat pounded faster.

"Has any man made you come on this kitchen counter?"

She pulled in a harsh breath. "Excuse me?"

"You heard me. Have any of your lovers made you come on this kitchen counter?"

He watched the silent war she fought with herself. Would she give in to the indignation she thought she should feel but really didn't? Would she answer him truthfully? Tell him a lie? Did she want to make him jealous or make herself feel better about what had transpired over the past six years?

Erik knew the answer to that question already. While she might consider it, Lola had never been a liar, even when she probably should have. And that same honesty wouldn't allow her to fabricate feelings she didn't really have even if her brain told her she should.

Which left them with the truth, exactly what he wanted.

"No."

"I'm about to change that."

Grasping her hips, Erik picked her up and set her onto the counter. He'd pushed away fantasies of doing this to her the first time he'd walked into her kitchen, had been good and kept his hands to himself. Tonight he was in no mood to deny himself or her.

They were a strange mix of familiar and unfamiliar. He knew when she was aroused because he'd memorized the way she looked when she wanted him years ago. But the actual thoughts spinning behind those deep brown eyes…they were lost to him now.

But he wanted to know them. Wanted to know everything about her, like he used to. When they were so close he'd thought nothing could come between them.

Erik reached for the hem of her shirt, pulled the garment off and tossed it behind him. Leaning close, he breathed deep, pulling the heady scent of her deep into his lungs and holding her there. Citrus and spice, something uniquely Lola. A memory that burst across his brain each time she came near.

Finding the sensitive curve where her throat met shoulder, Erik latched on and sucked. He relished her sharp indrawn breath and the groan she tried desperately to stifle. Some things were definitely the same.

Sweeping her hair out of the way, he found the catch of her bra. He flicked the clasp open, and his fingertips scraped across her skin as he dragged the straps down and away.

She was so beautiful. Not perfect—no one was— but the way she was put together sent him to his knees every damn time.

Her golden skin glowed in the moonlight. A riot of dark curls with those cheeky blue streaks rained down her back and across her shoulders. Soft and wild, just like the woman.

Threading his fingers into it and tilting her head backward, Erik stared into her eyes for several seconds, searching. For what, he wasn't sure. Uncertainty, maybe. Or a spark of what used to be there.

Tonight her gaze held neither, at least not that she would let him see. There was heat and a ribbon of nervous energy he recognized because it flowed through him, as well.

"Tell me you want this." It was a question even if he hadn't phrased it as one. An opportunity for her to tell him to stop.

Lola's gaze bounced around his face—eyes, mouth, chin—and back to his eyes. She reached for him, her fingertips ghosting across the edge of his jaw. How could a touch so light feel so good?

And then she was holding him still, reaching for him, whispering, "I want this," right before her mouth melded with his.

The kiss spun away from him within the space of a breath. As if he'd ever had control of it to begin with. Nothing else mattered except the feel of Lola's lips against his. The gentle suck as she pulled his tongue into her mouth and took what she wanted. His grip on her hips tightened, scooting her closer.

She pulled his shirt off, her hands on him feeling so damn good. Perfect. Right in a way he'd never experienced with anyone else, no matter how hard he'd tried to find it.

Stepping back, he popped the button on her shorts and helped her push the rest of her clothes onto the floor.

Erik dropped to his knees between her spread thighs. Perched on her counter, Lola stared down at him, an angel from on high.

Moonlight streamed through the wide windows, gilding her and making her radiant.

If he could figure out how to bottle her energy, drive and charisma, he could be a millionaire. Lola had always possessed the ability to draw people to her. To make them feel comfortable and safe.

She'd done that for him since the first day he'd met her. A feat that was unbelievable.

He'd missed the way she made him feel. He'd missed the reality of the man she'd always seen he could be. With her, Erik had felt strong enough to conquer the world and sure enough to accomplish anything.

He hadn't felt that in years, not since he'd walked away from her. Since then, he'd been floundering. No place felt right. Not the way she did.

Tonight, he not only wanted that back but also wanted to show her just how much he worshipped the woman she'd become.

Running his hands up the inside of her thighs, Erik pressed until she opened wider for him. The scent of her arousal hit him, heady and perfect. He'd done that to her, made her achy and wet.

A surge of possessive power shot through him.

His mouth followed his fingers, nipping and licking the soft skin of her inner thighs.

"Erik," she murmured, running her fingers through his hair.

His fingers played across the lips of her sex. Spreading her open, he relished the slippery evidence that she wanted him just as much as he wanted her.

His name turned into a moan in the back of her throat when his thumb brushed lightly across her swollen clit. Not enough to relieve the pressure, just enough to inflame the ache.

And then he leaned forward to let the tip of his tongue trail lazily from the entrance to her sex up to that needy bundle of nerves. Over and over, he took the same path, savoring the salty taste of her as it filled his mouth. She squirmed and panted, lifted her hips and urged him to give her more, touch her harder. "Dammit, Erik, *do* something."

He chuckled against her skin, letting the vibration of the sound become another source of torture. "Patience, Lo. I am."

Her fingers threaded into his hair, gripping hard and trying to force him into action. Even prone at her feet, he wouldn't give in to her. Not when he was enjoying this so damn much.

Her entire body was trembling with need. Her lungs heaved because she couldn't catch her breath. Her pupils were so wide Erik was pretty sure he could see the entire universe in her gaze.

And that was precisely where he wanted her. For now. Where he wanted her most was wrapped tight in his arms.

Deciding they'd both had enough, Erik drove two fingers deep inside her at the same time his mouth latched on to her clit and sucked. Lola's keening cry split the quiet night. Her entire body bucked beneath him and then shattered.

Deep inside, he felt the rhythmic motion of her muscles, caught up in the throes of the orgasm just like the rest of her. His own erection, rock hard and throbbing with a ceaseless cadence of his blood, jerked as he thought of being buried deep inside her, being milked to his own relief.

He nearly went off in his pants like he was a damn teenager.

Erik stayed with her, pulling out every last speck of sensation until Lola collapsed backward onto the wide, island counter. Arm flung over her face, she tried to close her thighs again, but Erik wasn't having any of that.

He wanted her just like this, spent, open and thoroughly satisfied.

Standing up, he stared down at her for several seconds. Her sweat-slicked skin glistened. Her lungs labored to pull in a full breath.

Eventually she dropped the arm from her face and stared up at him.

"Hi," he said.

Her mouth twisted into a grin that she quickly pulled into a rueful expression. "Wipe that satisfied smirk from your face right now."

"I don't think so. Besides, I'm pretty sure I'm not the one who was just satisfied."

"If you're trying to guilt me into sucking you off, it's not going to work."

Erik felt his expression sober. "You know me better than that, Lola. I enjoyed doing that. I like getting my mouth on you."

"It doesn't hurt that you're arrogant and like the sound of your name."

Her words were harsh, but her fingers threaded through his, pulling him a little closer.

"Baby, I only like it when you scream it."

She harrumphed but didn't have an immediate smart-mouthed comeback. So Erik used their tangled fingers to pull her upright. He urged her to the end of the counter, walked into the open V of her thighs and boosted her up until she wrapped her legs around his waist.

The heat of her sex nestled right over the long ridge of his aching erection. One thin layer of well-worn denim was all that separated him from sliding home deep inside her. God, he wanted that more than his next breath.

"What are you doing?" she asked.

"Taking you to bed, obviously."

"I'm capable of walking there myself."

"Maybe, but I'm not ready to take my hands off you."

She stiffened in his arms and then relaxed, burying her face into his throat as she wrapped her arms around his neck.

The soft bursts of her breath tickled his skin, sending goose bumps scattering over his body.

Out of nowhere, she murmured, "I like sucking you off. Watching your eyes go glassy and blank. The harsh sounds you make in the back of your throat. The taste and feel of you against my tongue."

Jesus, was she trying to send him to his knees? "Yeah, baby, I know."

She did. Some women didn't like it at all, but she enjoyed it, at least with him. That kind of enthusiasm was hard to fake. He understood the appeal, the thrill of giving your partner pleasure any way they wanted and enjoyed it.

"But I'm too tired to do that tonight," she said.

"It's okay."

She shook her head, sending her gorgeous cloud of hair dancing. "No, it isn't. I want to. I've been thinking about getting you in my mouth for weeks."

She was definitely trying to kill him. "Later. We have plenty of time."

The minute the words were out, Erik realized they weren't true. For the first time since coming home, the thought of leaving again hurt. He had a good life in California. A job he loved and was great at. Coworkers and friends who meant something to him. He should *want* to go back.

Yes, Sweetheart held a lot for him, too, but he hadn't even contemplated the possibility of staying.

Now…now he really needed to consider it. And not just because of the baby.

If he and Lola had any chance of picking the pieces back up, didn't they both deserve that opportunity? She couldn't come to him, but he could stay.

Was that the right thing to do?

Erik had no idea. And he probably shouldn't be making that kind of decision with Lola's naked, replete body wrapped around him. Especially considering his dick was still throbbing.

"Catnap. Let me nap and then I'll be back in fighting form."

Oh, Erik had no doubt. It was a rarity when Lola wasn't in fighting form, ready to tackle anyone and anything. Her ceaseless drive was one of her best qualities… and most frustrating.

Reaching her bedroom, Erik pulled back the covers, placed her on the mattress and snuggled the blankets up around her shoulders. He turned to walk away, but she held out her hand.

"Stay."

A million thoughts rushed through his brain. Most important: was this the smart thing to do? Shrugging the second thoughts back for another time, he shed the rest of his own clothes and climbed into bed beside her.

Already half-asleep, Lola rolled until she was pressed against his side. Her body draped over his. It took her no time to drop the rest of the way to sleep. He could tell the moment she did, her body melting into his.

Between his unhappy erection and the thoughts spinning through his head, it should have taken him forever to fall asleep. But it didn't. He was out in minutes, dreaming of the past and his subconscious building a future he was afraid to trust outside sleep.

9

THE LAST FEW days had been surreal. When had Lola lost control of her own life? There was a part of her completely pissed about that reality. The rest of her… couldn't quite work up the energy to care.

With Erik and Colt colluding together against her, her schedule was a thing of beauty and included mandatory nap periods every afternoon. Lola had to admit—reluctantly—that she appreciated those thirty minutes. By the time her nap rolled around, she was always dragging, but even after just a little catnap, she felt rejuvenated and ready to tackle the rest of her day.

Although she'd never tell either of them that, it *was* rather efficient. Left to her own devices, she'd have tried to power through until the point she physically couldn't handle anymore. And then lose hours instead of thirty minutes.

But it wasn't just the naps. The feeling of losing control had crept into other aspects of her life. Her brother had started shopping online for baby furniture. Her brother! Sending her links to sites with cute nursery ideas that would have had her ovaries weeping with envy if they hadn't already done their job and gotten her pregnant.

She hadn't even had her first doctor's appointment yet—although she was taking prenatal vitamins and had one scheduled—and already her entire life seemed to be shifting focus.

And while she'd never really thought about having a child and how that would change everything, she had to admit she liked it. She'd even plunked down over a grand on a beautiful crib that should arrive in the next three to four weeks.

A vision of Erik assembling the pieces had invaded her brain, but she'd purposely pushed the thought away. That was a dangerous and pointless road to travel down. He wouldn't be here when it arrived. They had less than one week before he was supposed to return to California.

Lola tried not to let the thoughts invade whenever he was close, but it was difficult. The more Erik integrated himself into her life, the harder she knew it would be when he left.

But even so, she couldn't find the strength to push him away. She'd adopted the philosophy of dealing with the inevitable when it actually happened. Something she'd no doubt regret when the piper came to collect.

Crossing the outskirts of the park at the center of town, Lola greeted the cluster of her friends and their spouses and kids. The sun had set a half hour ago, bringing the scorching summer heat down closer to something bearable.

On the far end of the park, a huge movie screen had been set up for the traditional movie in the park that seemed to be a Southern staple. Tonight they were showing a double feature, a kid favorite about an ice princess and a parent flick about a group of guys driving fast cars.

Lola didn't really care what was on the screen. She was simply looking forward to a night out with her friends.

Behind her, Erik set up their lawn chairs, the same ones he'd refused to let her carry even though they weighed about two pounds. He popped the top on a bottle of water and, without interrupting her conversation with Hope, slipped the bottle into her hand. Lola tossed him a grateful smile as she took a strong pull. The cold liquid felt wonderful on her dry throat.

Around her, the chaos of her group settled deep beneath her skin. Hope and Gage's twin girls, three years old now, weaved in and out of the forest of adult legs, yelling to each other in the twin language only the two of them understood. Lexi was crouched on the ground, letting her son, who'd just learned to walk, toddle around even as she craned her neck backward to stay part of a conversation with Willow and Tatum. Dev, Willow's husband, and Evan pushed absently at their own strollers.

These were her people, and she couldn't discount how amazing it was going to be to raise her son or daughter alongside these men and women. She'd have been lying if she said she hadn't felt a burst of fear the moment she found out she was pregnant. She had no idea how to do this. It was times like those that she missed her mother so much. That hole felt like it went straight through her soul. But she had great examples in the women around her. She and her baby would be okay.

One of the twins tripped. Without even hesitating, Evan reached out and caught the back of her shirt before she could connect with the ground. As he swung her up into the air, the little girl's laughter pealed through the noise. He dropped her down and blew a raspberry on her belly before saying, "Be careful, precious."

"I will, Unca Ev," she promised with her little girl lisp as he set her back down. They weren't actually related, but that didn't matter. Evan had been a part of the child's life from the moment she was born.

Erik wandered over to Dev and Evan, easily slipping into their conversation. He'd only met them both during this trip, but they all seemed like old friends. Lola eyed him for several moments, but his body language clearly said he was relaxed.

Gage and Blake joined them, and within a few minutes, Lola found herself surrounded by their wives and bombarded with questions.

"How are you feeling?" Willow asked.

"Colt told Dev that you're cutting back your hours a bit for the next couple months. That's smart."

"So, what the heck is going on between you and Erik? You both seem pretty comfortable with each other." Tatum drawled.

The natural noise of five women carrying on simultaneous conversations ground to a halt as every pair of eyes zeroed in on her, waiting for an answer to the last question, which she wasn't prepared to give.

"Um…nothing," Lola said, though she was sure they could see through her and they weren't going to let her get away with it.

"He had his hand on the small of your back as you both walked up." Hope pointed out.

Lexi chimed in, "He opened your water."

"And according to the Sweetheart rumor mill, his truck has been outside your house several nights this week. All night." Tatum's eyebrows waggled suggestively.

Lola couldn't fight the blush that heated up her skin. Yeah, it wasn't the first time she and Erik had been grist for that rumor mill but… She shifted uncomfortably in her seat.

"Woo-hoo, someone's getting laid!" Hope exclaimed.

Exasperation finally surfaced, trumping the chagrin she shouldn't have felt in the first place. She and Erik were both adults, dammit. "Don't give me that, Hope Harper. You make it sound like I'm the only one in the entire city having sex. I know for a fact you all get laid on the regular." She pointedly let her gaze sweep across the crop of kids surrounding them.

Willow gave a soft, serene smile and then blew them all out of the water with, "I can't speak for the rest of you, but Dev and I had to pull over on the way here."

Hope grumbled. "Darn kids old enough to ask questions. Enjoy the days of quickies while you can," she said, pointing at Willow with a lemon square from Lexi's bakery.

"Oh, there was nothing quick about it," Willow drawled, flashing a satisfied grin.

"But we're getting off track here," Lexi said, pulling everyone's attention back where Lola didn't want it. "Seriously, we know that things with Erik are complicated, and we're just worried about you. What's going on?"

Lola's gaze traveled over to the knot of guys. She couldn't keep her gaze from trailing down Erik's body, taking in the curve of his tight ass and the broad expanse of his shoulders along the way. Lust, strong and insistent, rolled through her, leaving a pleasant buzz deep in her blood.

"Oh, yeah, she's lost."

Shaking her head, Lola forced herself to look back at her friends. "I don't know. Really. The attraction and chemistry have always been there, and we just decided to stop fighting it."

"That's good." Lexi nodded.

"No, that's bad," she countered. "Because he's leaving in a few days. We're just…" Lola looked up at the stars, fighting the sting at the back of her eyes. "…playing house for the moment. I can't count on him. I learned that lesson the hard way once already."

There. She'd said it out loud. Voiced her biggest fear and her truest reality.

"Oh, sweetheart," Hope murmured. "Maybe that's not how it will go down. Is there any way he might decide to stay?"

Lola wasn't going there. Couldn't allow herself to wish for something that wasn't on the table. Shaking her head vigorously, she said, "No."

Because it wasn't happening.

Wrapping her arms around her, Hope pulled her into a rough hug. "I'm so sorry. You know we're here for you, anytime, any way."

Yeah, she did know that. "I'll deal when I need to. Until then, I'm going to enjoy whatever this is because I know the next few months—and years—are going to be hectic."

Hope squeezed her shoulders. "You're not wrong, but it'll be totally worth it."

The conversation turned to other things—life, kids, jobs and businesses. Lola stayed a part of the chatter, but on the outskirts as she let the comfort of it all wash over her. Somewhere in the middle of a musical number with a snowman, Lola looked back over to the guys and had to do a double take to make sure she was seeing correctly.

Erik held Bradley, Dev and Willow's four-month-old son. Erik cradled him against his chest, his hand moving rhythmically across the child's back. He rocked on the balls of his feet, back and forth, even as he continued whatever conversation he was a part of.

Willow leaned over to Lola. "He looks good holding Brad."

Yeah, he did. Lola had always known he'd be a good dad, if for no other reason than that he was determined not to make the mistakes his own father had. But seeing him like this…he seemed so comfortable and capable.

When had that happened?

Lola was up out of her chair before she could process her intentions. Crossing the space, she slipped behind Erik, letting her hand trail across his hip even as she peered around his shoulder.

Looking down at her, he smiled. "Shh, he's back asleep."

An angelic little face, scrunched in sleep, greeted her. Brad was one of the cutest babies she'd ever seen.

"How'd you learn to do that?" she asked, her voice low so as not to wake him.

"Put a baby to sleep? One of my friends back home has triplets. When they were born a year ago, it was all hands on deck, including mine. I really wasn't interested in learning how to diaper and bottle-feed. My plan had been to contribute by buying wipes and meals and shit. But the first night I showed up after shift, Wes greeted me at the door with a squalling bundle in each arm and this *save me* expression on his face." Erik shrugged.

"So you stepped up."

A stain of color spread up his neck and across his cheeks. That was almost as endearing as the story he'd just told her. "I guess."

"Boys or girls?"

"Two boys and a girl. All a handful, although she's the worst. Already knows how to flash those big, bright eyes and get what she wants out of everyone around her, even me."

Lola had to laugh at the mental image of some cherubic toddler wrapping a big, bad firefighter around her little finger. "Do you want a boy or a girl?"

Lola hadn't meant to ask the question. It just popped out. She wasn't even sure that she knew what she wanted yet.

Erik's expression was bright and fathomless as he craned his neck to look at her. "I've always wanted a little girl, with your gorgeous chocolate eyes, warm skin and larger-than-life laugh. One with the same spark of attitude, even though I know it'll drive us both crazy while she's young. Totally worth it if she grows into half the woman her mother is."

Aww, hell. Twisting, Lola pressed her face against Erik's arm and drew in a deep, steadying breath.

She was in trouble. So much trouble. She could feel her heart trembling with joy and fear. She wanted so much to believe they could find their way back to what they'd had before. But putting her faith in that...

She wasn't ready to take that risk. Not again. It had left her spinning for months. Years. If she was honest, she'd still been spinning when Erik showed up here all those weeks ago. She'd been unable to give any other man a chance because none of them measured up to *him*. Even with all his flaws, even after walking away from her and her brother when they needed him most.

Erik was dangerous and she was in over her head.

THE EVENING HAD been great. He really liked Lola's friends. He'd known a few of them, but since he was a couple of years older, they'd never been close. She'd gathered a great group of people around her, and that made him happy.

He liked knowing there were people who had her

back when and if she needed it. She had that in her family, too, but friends were different and just as important. Sometimes more so, since they usually were right alongside you for the fun and trouble.

He loved watching her laugh. There was something about the sparkle in her eyes that just made his entire chest tight and open at the same time.

At one point, she'd crawled onto the ground to play with the twins. She was a natural with the kids, but that didn't surprise him.

What did was the way she'd leaned against him, wrapping her arms around his knee and placing her head in his lap. It was a comfortable gesture, one neither of them would have thought twice about six years ago.

Tonight, it was a symbol that he took to heart. Weaving his fingers through her thick hair, Erik massaged her scalp down into the long column of her neck.

"Mmm," she murmured, arching into his touch like a cat.

The movie played on the screen across the park, but none of them seemed to be paying it any attention. Slowly the kids lost the fight with sleep, and before long they were all out. The twins were adorable, arms wrapped around each other, foreheads pressed together, like they'd nodded off midconversation.

The adults drifted together in pairs. Hope climbed into Gage's lap, curling up and resting her head on his shoulder. Dev, lying on the blanket he'd spread out, wrapped a hand around Willow's calf and urged her down beside him, tucking her body into the curve of his own. Evan plopped his butt onto the grass in front of

Tatum's chair and wiggled backward until she opened her legs and let him lean against her, threading her fingers through his hair. Lexi and Blake sat side by side, but their heads were leaned together as they murmured softly to each other.

Erik's chest seized with jealousy at the sight of all these couples surrounding them.

This was what had been missing in his life. He'd watched the same thing with the guys he worked beside, never admitting it bothered him to be the single guy among the couples when they held family barbecues or invited him over to watch a game. Their wives and girlfriends had tried to set him up with friends, coworkers and—in one really bad blind date experience— a dog groomer.

None of the women had worked out because none of them had been Lola. Without meaning to, he'd compared each and every one of them to her. None had her exuberance or confidence. Her soft hair or warm eyes. Her ability to call him on his bullshit because she'd known him forever.

Resting her head on his thigh, Lola rolled so that she could look up at him. Light from the screen flickered across her face, and in that moment she'd never looked more beautiful. She hadn't bothered with makeup or fancy clothes. Her toes, tipped with red polish, wiggled in the grass, her feet bare because she'd tossed her flip-flops underneath his chair.

She was perfectly Lola and he loved her.

It was that simple. He always had and he always would.

"Take me home?" she asked, staring up at him through sleepy, sultry eyes. It was a strange combination that stirred in him a need to kiss the hell out of her and scoop her up into his arms to protect her at the same time.

"Anytime, gorgeous," he murmured.

Quietly they gathered their things and whispered farewells to everyone.

He grasped her hand and pulled her close as they weaved their way through the scattered people back to his truck. The drive to her place was quiet and cozy. He kept hold of her, stroking his thumb across the back of her hand because he needed to touch her.

Lola started to unpack everything from the back of his truck, but grasping her gently by the waist, Erik pulled her away. "Leave it. It'll be here in the morning."

"But…" Lola turned slightly, ready to protest, but as she got a good look at him, something hot flared in her eyes. "Okay," she said, twisting fully into him.

Her hands landed on his chest and her face turned up to his, expectant, waiting. He wondered if she could feel the erratic beat of his heart beneath her palms.

Laying his own over hers, Erik kept her right there as she backed slowly up the walk to her front door. He had to release her to unlock it and let them in, but the minute they were inside, Erik pressed her against the wall.

She sucked in a sharp breath but never took her gaze off him. He wanted to devour her. Instead, he leaned down and settled a soft kiss against her lush lips. The vibration of her moan was his reward.

He teased and savored, gradually deepening the kiss

until her sighs and his low groans melded together. Her fingers found him, skimming up and down his body in an unhurried need to explore.

This slow exploration was what he wanted tonight. They'd been blinded by passion for days, but this felt like a reawakening, a thorough rediscovery and building of so much more. Something had changed tonight—with him or with her, Erik wasn't certain. But right now, they had no need to hurry. He wanted to learn every nuance of her. He wanted to remember.

Slowly she bunched the hem of his shirt in her hands and dragged it over his head. Dipping close, she let her mouth trail lazily across his skin, laving and worshipping in a way that drove him insane even as it freed something deep inside him.

"You're unbelievable, Erik. So perfect and strong. You constantly amaze me." She peppered his body with kisses and words of praise that soothed wounds he hadn't even realized still reverberated with pain and remorse.

Wrapping her hair through his fingers, he used his hold to pull her head back so he could look into her eyes. "No, you're the amazing one. Lola, you're fearless and always have been."

A shaky laugh burst through her parted lips. "Hardly. I'm scared every single day. I'm scared right now. But that doesn't matter anymore."

He wanted to ask her what she was scared of but didn't want to lose the moment. And wasn't sure he was ready to hear the answer.

Shaking her head, she said, "Maybe we should move this mutual admiration society to the bedroom."

A burst of laughter shot through him. "Whatever the lady wants."

Lola grinned and wrapped her arms around his neck when he swung her up into the air. "Erik," she said in a breathless voice, but he wasn't sure if the single word was an admonishment or delight. He wasn't sure Lola knew, either.

Crawling across the bed, he deposited her into the center, pushing off the mound of pillows she insisted on using.

Knees bent, feet flat on the bed and propped up onto her elbows, Lola watched him shrug out of his clothes. The heat from her gaze set his body on fire, a roiling need that he wasn't sure could ever be extinguished. Did he really want it to be?

Never.

Reaching for her ankle, Erik slowly trailed his fingers up the soft line of her legs, dipping just beneath the hem of her shorts. A hiss slipped between her teeth even as she arched into his caress, silently asking for more.

Taking her clothes off was like unwrapping the best Christmas present, the one he'd spent years asking for. Only he got to do it again and again, filled with that giddy excitement each time.

He flicked the button on her waistband, tugged at her zipper and then pulled her shorts and panties down her legs. He followed the trail back up with his mouth, enjoying her soft sighs of pleasure. But he didn't touch the close-cropped mound of curls at the top, not even when her hips pulsed up in silent demand.

Instead, he moved his attention to her loose, flowing shirt, not bothering to open the row of tiny white buttons, just pulling it off. Urging her shoulders up off the bed, Erik pressed his palm to the middle of her back to support her even as he flicked open the clasp of her bra. He flattened his palm just below the band, spreading his fingers to keep the cups in place.

Latching his mouth onto the sensitive curve of her neck, Erik licked and sucked his way across her collarbone until he reached the strap settled against her shoulder. With his lips, he nudged it down, following it with nipping kisses and his trailing tongue. He stopped to suck on the inside of her elbow and again at her wrist, enjoying the way her pulse fluttered beneath his mouth.

He paid the same attention to the other side, finally lifting his hand and letting her bra fall away. "Erik, you're killing me," she whispered.

"No, love, I promise I'm not."

He, on the other hand, might die from sheer loss of blood to his brain. Erik was pretty sure every drop in his body had gone south to his pounding erection.

When she was finally naked, Erik pushed back onto his heels. Kneeling between her open thighs, he had the perfect view of Lola, spread out like a banquet before him. He wanted to taste every inch of her. Know every part of her.

Her sex glistened with desire, begging him to bring them together, bury himself deep inside her.

Lifting her arms up, Lola beckoned to him. "Come

here." And he couldn't deny either of them any longer. Erik positioned himself at the opening of her sex.

He planned to take it slow, but Lola had other ideas. Pushing up into him, she begged, "Hurry," spreading wide and pulling him in several inches.

And that was all she wrote. A single taste of her heat surrounding him and everything else faded to nothing. He couldn't stop his hips from driving forward, from claiming her with one, sure thrust.

Lola's back arched, her eyes closing in bliss. "God, yes."

Nope, that wasn't going to work for him. "Lola, look at me." He wanted her eyes on him as they came together and fell apart.

She obeyed, finding his gaze with her own ecstasy-blurred stare. Pleasure suffused her skin, making it glow and burn. Erik leaned down and nipped at her jaw, lips and throat even as he thrust in and out.

He found a rhythm so good he struggled to keep his eyes from rolling back into his head. He wouldn't give in to the impulse, not when he wanted to watch Lola break apart in his arms.

Her hands skittered over his body, aimless and needy. Like she wanted any piece of him she could get. A feeling Erik understood all too well because he wanted the same thing.

The hot clasp of her sex clenched tight around him. He could feel the flutters deep inside as her body strained for the orgasm they both craved.

"Erik. Oh, God. Erik," she panted. Again and again, their bodies connected, spiraling higher and higher. He could see Lola's urgency and determination, her greedy need for more, and didn't blame her. He'd have given anything to make these moments with her last forever.

"Let go, Lola."

She shook her head, her wild curls spinning up in a cloud around them. "Too good," she groaned.

Her nails clawed into his shoulder, drawing pain and probably blood. Reaching back for her, he tangled their fingers together, ignoring her whimper when he had to stop for a few seconds.

Bringing their joined hands beside her head, he changed the angle of his hips and stroked long and sure inside her. Lola's entire body tightened, and she couldn't stifle the guttural noise that erupted.

She stared at him through sightless eyes, her mouth forming silent, begging words that he wanted to hear and feel.

"Lola, come," he demanded, plunging deep.

She trembled, teetering at the edge of an abyss for several breathless seconds before finally tipping over. Every muscle in her body contracted and then pulsed in wave after wave of bliss.

Her sex clamped tight around him, massaging him in a way he couldn't fight. His own orgasm tingled up from his toes and exploded out of his brain, or at least it felt that way. Everything went black before bright colors burst across his vision.

Erik didn't remember collapsing onto the bed beside Lola. Or gathering her up into his arms as she mewled softly beside him, her body still quivering from after-shocks that rocked him, too.

He wasn't sure how long they stayed that way—long enough for sweat to dry and leave his skin chilled. Finally Lola pushed onto her elbows. Curls fell into her face. Reaching up, Erik smoothed them back so he could see her.

She stared at him, a little dazed. But there was something familiar in her gaze. Emotion that made his gut twist with a hope he was so afraid of feeling.

Because he didn't deserve it. He didn't deserve her. But the more time he spent with Lola, the more he began to worry that no longer mattered.

He'd walked away from her once because it was the right thing to do—for her, for him.

Could she forgive him? Could they forget the past?

God, he wanted that…but he just didn't know.

10

LOLA WOKE UP with a strange energy buzzing beneath her skin. It roughly resembled joy, but that couldn't be from falling asleep and waking up next to Erik. She'd done that several times now.

It was funny. They'd never actually done much sleeping in the same bed when they were dating. She'd still lived at home, commuting to college in Charleston for the first couple of years to save money and be close to him. She'd moved after Erik left because she'd needed the change of scenery to help her adjust.

Waking up beside him could seriously become addictive. The warmth of him wrapped around her, his scent even better than the smell of coffee. And hardly anything topped coffee.

Which was why Lola forced herself to get out of bed and start her day. But even that felt…strangely normal. The two of them shared the bathroom, and their movements as they scooted around each other felt like a well-choreographed routine they'd been practicing for years.

Without any real discussion, Erik followed her out the door, dropped a kiss onto her mouth and then watched as she pulled out of the driveway. Because he'd mentioned it last night, she knew he intended to spend some time with his mom today before heading over to the station to see the guys. He'd picked up a shift tomorrow, so afterward he would probably end up sleeping at his mom's place instead of hers. He didn't want to disturb her when he got up early.

Lola tried not to let disappointment creep in. This was a good thing. They needed some time apart. In fact, that was what she was going to do with today. Clear her head and get it back on straight.

Because last night had been...intense. In a way that had felt much bigger than anything they'd ever shared before. When Erik was close, he was all she could think of, all she could see, hear and taste.

But that wasn't smart. She was falling head over heels.

There, she'd admitted it.

Which was also pretty stupid. So...she needed distance.

She had a full slate with two toddler shoots this morning followed by a senior portrait session in the afternoon and her first doctor's appointment sandwiched between.

Her first appointment.

Even the thought of it made her slightly giddy. She knew, in every fiber of her being, that she was pregnant. She felt it to her core and had several pink lines on test sticks to prove it. But a small part of her wouldn't quite believe it until she heard the doctor talk about due dates and prenatal care.

The morning flew by, and for the first time in days, she wasn't dragged down by exhaustion, which, considering how she'd spent her evening, was surprising. Maybe earth-shattering sex was the key she'd been missing to feeling good.

She got some amazingly beautiful and adorable shots with the kids at each session and even managed to convince one mom to get into the frame. Lola was excited to share the exuberance and love that she'd captured from behind her lens.

She was packing her camera back into the protective case when Colt rolled into the room. "If you don't leave in the next fifteen minutes, you're going to be late. Is Erik meeting you at the doctor's office?"

Lola glanced up, but went immediately back to what she was doing. "Erik isn't coming."

"What?" Colt's voice boomed through the room. "Why the hell wouldn't he want to come to your first appointment? I'm going to kick his ass."

"Simmer down, Ali. No one's kicking any ass today. He isn't coming because I didn't tell him."

Colt rolled closer, bumping her softly on the leg with the edge of his chair. It was a trick he used when he wanted her undivided attention. "Excuse me?"

She shrugged, glancing at her brother and then away again. Guilt she didn't want to feel burst through her. "I didn't tell him. Look, the reality is, he'll be leaving soon, and I'll be doing this mostly on my own. Better to start out the way I plan to continue."

After last night she'd needed breathing room.

"Better for whom, Lola Marie? Not Erik. Not the baby."

Lola yanked the zipper on her camera bag and shoved it away from her, grateful for the protective layers inside when it skidded off the other end of the table and toppled to the floor.

"Don't judge me, Colt. I'm doing the best I can here with a less than ideal situation."

"Maybe you should have thought of that before you let Erik spend the night at your house all week."

Lola dropped her head back. She didn't need this. Not right now. Spearing her brother with a sharp gaze, she said, "He's the one who left, Colt. And he's the one who'll leave again. I was shattered before. I'll do whatever I need to in order to keep myself from ending up worse this time."

A strangled sob vibrated through her throat. She hadn't been aware it was coming but somehow managed to keep it from erupting.

"Lo," Colt whispered, running his hands down her arms. "Maybe it's time to forgive him for his mistake six years ago and give him the benefit of the doubt."

She shook her head. "I can't do that, Colt." Her words were thick with tears. "If I do, I won't be leaving myself anywhere to hide when this goes south. And it will. We both know he'll leave. Maybe not in a few days, but eventually. That's what he's good at now, right?"

Colt's mouth thinned, and an unhappy line formed between his brows. "That was a long time ago, Lo. Maybe he's changed, grown up. He has you and a baby on the way, two good reasons to deal with the demons chasing him."

"That's not what you said several days ago."

Colt shook his head, sadness filling his eyes. "What I said several days ago was my attempt to protect you, Lo. But you made a choice to let him back in. That has consequences...for you and for him."

No. She couldn't listen to this. Not right now. She was too vulnerable to let hope take root and bloom. "He left, Colt. Not just me, but you. When you needed him most. I can't trust him to be here for me, for my family."

Wrapping his arms around her waist, Colt pulled her down until she was curled up in his lap, her head cradled against his shoulder.

"That man has always loved you, Lola. Never once have I doubted that. I think, more than concentrating on how he failed us, maybe it's time to ask how we failed him."

Lola reared back, staring at her brother like he'd grown two heads. "Are you insane? You were lying in a hospital bed, one he was at least partly responsible for putting you in. Exactly how did we fail him?"

Colt squeezed her hand. "My accident was not his fault, Lola. I made my own decision that night, a decision I would make again and again even knowing the outcome. I don't blame him, so why do you?"

She sniffed. She'd heard Colt and her father yelling about what happened that night, both of them angry at themselves and each other. Her father had given a direct order that both Colt and Erik ignored, returning to a building on the verge of collapse because a sobbing eight-year-old covered in soot stood on the sidewalk, knowing his father was trapped inside. They'd rescued the man, Erik carrying him to safety. Colt had been right behind him, but not close enough to avoid being hit by debris when the roof finally gave way.

Her father had been miserable and angry. Colt had been resigned and strong, accepting the consequences of his own actions with a resilience that often baffled Lola.

To hear him say he wouldn't change anything made her so proud and angry at the same time.

That night, her brother and boyfriend had sacrificed so much to save a father. They'd made the choice knowing what could happen.

Lola's problem was, they weren't the only ones who'd sacrificed that night. And the rest of them had no choice in the matter.

"He's hurting, Lo, and has been for years. I was lucky. I had you and Dad. My doctors and counselors. Erik, because he felt guilty and still does, ripped himself away from everyone who could help him deal with what happened. Have you ever wondered why he threw himself into a job that has a high statistical risk of injury and death? And after he left Sweetheart, hell, Lo, he went out and found the single most dangerous thing he could do with the experience he already had.

"And we let him leave. None of us went after him. Not you, not me, not Dad. He was a part of our family for years but we let him just walk away. When I was spiraling down into depression, lashing out and drinking too much, what did you do?"

She'd knocked some sense into him, literally. Tossing an empty beer can at his head in a fit of anger that she was still embarrassed about. But her actions had finally worked and he'd gotten help. Agreed to counseling and found a direction for his life that she would forever be grateful for.

"Exactly," he murmured. "But no one did that for him. Which only reinforced his idea that he didn't deserve to be rescued."

Shit.

Colt's words ripped straight through her. They tore at her defenses and arguments, leaving her heart wide open and vulnerable.

Because she knew he was right.

Pulling her down again, Colt pressed a kiss to her forehead. "Enough deep thoughts for today. You have an appointment to get to."

ERIK WALKED INTO the studio. The space always made him smile because it was just so Lola. Eclectic and beautiful. He could see touches of her personality in the beige-and-turquoise walls, a perfect backdrop to the photographs that always seemed to be changing.

"Be right with you," Colt hollered from the back.

"No rush, man. I'm here to take Lola to lunch."

Colt rolled down the hallway and into the open, airy front room. "Is she aware of that?" he asked, a single eyebrow disappearing into his hairline in a question that already seemed to have an answer.

"No, I wanted to surprise her," Erik said, drawing out the words because he was starting to feel that might not have been a smart idea.

"Oh, she's going to be surprised," Colt said, his mouth twisting. "But then, I guess you will be, too."

His dry words hinted this surprise wasn't going to be a good one. "Where is she?"

"At the doctor's."

Everything in Erik stilled and then went blazing fast. He started to grab for his keys in his pocket. "Why the hell didn't someone call me? What's wrong? Where?"

"Calm down, man. She's fine, and as far as I know, the baby is, too. She had her first appointment with the ob-gyn today."

"What?"

Erik's eyebrows slammed together, and his brain spun. They'd showered together this morning. Shared breakfast and gotten dressed in the same room. Not once did she mention having an appointment today.

Why the hell wouldn't she have told him?

Erik didn't realize he'd voiced the question aloud until Colt answered.

"Because she's scared shitless, Erik. She's afraid to let you into any part of her life because if she does, she's going to fall in love with you all over again and get her heart broken."

Well, hell. What was he supposed to say to that?

This whole thing scared him, too. But he'd thought they were navigating their way through. Last night he'd never felt closer to her. Closer to anyone, really. And that was saying a lot, considering how close they'd been years ago.

But this time…there was something different in the

way they'd interacted. Something deeper than had been there when they started dating as teenagers.

That had meant a lot to him. But apparently, not to her. Or not enough.

"I can see the storm brewing in that brain of yours," Colt said. "And you might not be in any frame of mind to listen to advice, but I'm gonna give it anyway. Talk to her. Don't yell and get angry. Talk to her."

Erik had no idea how that was going to work. He could feel the anger, mixed with a healthy dose of hurt, filling his chest, ready to explode.

Maybe if he'd had a few minutes to calm down, he could have found some reason, but when the bell above the door chimed and he turned to see Lola walking into the studio, any hope he'd had of getting a grasp on his temper evaporated.

"Erik. What are you doing here? I didn't expect to see you until tonight." Her breezy tone was more than he could take.

"Obviously. Is that when you were going to tell me about your appointment?"

Lola's gaze jerked to Colt's, her eyes narrowing with accusation.

Her brother held up his hands. "Don't give me that look. He came to take you to lunch. I wasn't going to lie to him."

"Of course not," she said, the words quick and unequivocal.

Colt's chair rolled back and then sideways as he headed for the front door. "I'm suddenly dying for a burger from the diner. I'll be back in…yeah, whenever

I think it's safe or the police show up, whichever happens first. Don't kill each other."

Erik didn't even bother to flick Colt a glance as he left, his gaze zeroed on Lola. "What the hell?" he asked, proud at the modulated tone he managed.

"Look, I just—" she whirled away, her arms crossing in front of her middle "—didn't want you there today, okay?"

"No, it isn't okay, Lola. I had a right to be there."

"No, no, you didn't." Her hand slapped over her mouth. "I didn't mean that," she mumbled around her fingers.

"Oh, I think you did. And I'm pretty sure it's the worst thing you've ever said to me."

A choked sound erupted from her throat. Sinking onto a nearby velvet couch, Lola dropped her head against its curved back, squeezing her eyes shut. "What are we doing, Erik?" she asked without even opening them.

When he didn't answer, she finally looked at him. The exhaustion and defeat stamped across every feature went a long way toward tempering his churning emotions.

"This," she wagged a finger between them. "What are we doing?"

It was pretty much the same question Colt had just asked him, and he didn't have any better answer now than he had a few minutes ago. "I don't know, Lola."

Her shoulders heaved on a silent sigh. "Yeah, that's what I'm afraid of. It nearly broke me when you left before. I can't… I just can't put everything I have into this unless I know it's not going to happen again. I understand this attitude isn't entirely fair, but that's the way it is. So, I need some lines and distance. This was my attempt to do that."

And cut him out of something they should both be sharing. "I'm sorry. I get it. I do. You make it sound like you're the only one carrying scars from what happened six years ago."

Her mouth twisted into a sickly smile. "Oh, I know I'm not, but I'm not sure that makes it any better. In fact, I'm pretty sure that makes it worse, since your wounds are self-inflicted. There was a time I would have sworn you'd stand beside me through anything. And then you left. So...yeah."

The hurt in her eyes tore him apart even more. He'd put it there, and he hated himself for that. Back then, he'd been fueled by selfish guilt and fear. He owed her a lot.

But not this.

"I'll give you whatever you need, Lola. But I can't let you cut me out of anything with the baby. That can't be the line you draw. This is nonnegotiable. I want to be part of the baby's life. Every part of it."

"And how are you planning to manage that from so far away?"

Erik shook his head. She had a point. They might have spent the last week jumping back into bed, but they'd actually done little to settle the issues between them.

They'd talked about their shared past. He'd told stories about his job and the places he'd lived. But they were both avoiding reality. Because neither of them knew the answer, did they?

He definitely didn't. Hell, that was true long before he'd arrived back in Sweetheart. Almost two months ago he'd lost a friend, gotten reckless and been placed on administrative leave. His life was spiraling before Lola had told him she was pregnant.

In fact, out of everything that had happened in the last few months, *that* was a bright spot. Something positive and exciting.

"Let me worry about how I'll manage being a dad," he finally ground out.

Lola laughed, the sound jarring and bitter. "Sure, because that's the kind of woman I am. I don't worry. Ever. Have you met me?" Lola leveled a pointed look in his direction. He couldn't help the bark of laughter that burst through his lips.

Not something he would have expected, given his red haze of anger just a few minutes ago.

Crouching down in front of her, he took both of her hands in his. They were so small. Lola's personality was so big that he often forgot she wasn't ten feet tall and bulletproof. For that matter, she seemed to forget it as well.

"This is something I won't compromise on. I want to be there, for you and the baby."

She bit her lip, worrying it for several seconds before reluctantly nodding.

"So, how did it go?" he asked.

"Good. Everything's on track. I'm due in late February."

He squeezed her hands and moved to stand up, but Lola's grip on him tightened, keeping him in place. "I'm sorry you weren't there."

"Me, too."

"It was actually overwhelming."

Erik realized just how much it cost Lola to admit that. She wasn't the kind of woman who routinely showed weakness, even to her closest friends.

"I mean, it was real before, but now it's *real*. There's an actual tiny human in there, depending on me for everything."

To Erik's surprise, she brought their linked hands to her belly and pressed his palm flat against it, as if she could transfer that knowledge to him through osmosis. "What if I'm awful at this?"

Lola's vulnerability nearly cut him at the knees.

Bending close, he stared her straight in the eye and told her the absolute truth. "You're going to be an amazing mom. A natural. You have the best family around you to help."

"But I don't have my mom." She ducked her head, but not before he could see the pain and regret filling her expression. "I wanted *her* there today, Erik."

Not him, but her mother. He understood, although that didn't stop the slight sting of her words. How many times had he dreamed of his dad showing up to watch his football games growing up? It never happened. He'd always known it wouldn't. But that didn't crush the need. The difference was, his father had chosen not to be involved.

"You have her example, Lola. And memories, good

memories. You have your family and some amazing friends." He wanted to add himself to the list, had to bite back the words. "You'll be fine. Better than fine. Amazing."

There was no part of him that didn't believe that. Lola would be a wonderful mom. Firm but loving. She'd laugh off the things that didn't matter but have no problem making the hard decisions, either.

He, on the other hand...

"If either of us is going to suck at this, it'll be me. But I was lucky enough to be a part of your family, so I have the same examples. We'll both be fine, Lola. No matter what happens, our baby is going to be loved by so many people."

And that was what mattered.

Erik carried plenty of scars. Being unwanted by a parent left damage no matter how good the support system around you was. There was always a part of you that wondered—what did you do wrong? What part of you was unworthy? What could you have changed or done differently?

Even if his adult brain *knew* the problem was his father's and not his, that didn't change the little boy inside he couldn't always silence. It was the same voice that had sent him running six years ago, certain that his actions had cost him the surrogate family who had adopted him.

Because how could it not? How could the man he'd looked to as a father not blame him for his son's accident when Erik blamed himself? How could Lola not see the damage he'd inflicted whenever she looked at him, just as he did when he looked at his reflection in the mirror?

Lola pushed back from him, her chocolate eyes bright. "You're going to be great at this, too. For years I watched you try to make up to your mom for the fact that your dad left. Something that wasn't your fault. You take on responsibiliies that aren't yours to shoulder. And that's not necessarily good. But in this case... I've always known it would make you an perfect father, because there's no part of you that would let your own child hurt the way you did."

God, her words slayed him.

She held his face still so she could look deep into his eyes. "I really am sorry. The minute the nurse called me back, I regretted not asking you to come with me."

Everything inside Erik wanted to accept her apology and let the whole thing go. But there was a part of him that just...couldn't. She'd taken something from him. More than that, she'd taken something from *them*. A shared moment there was no way ever to get back.

Just this morning he'd been contemplating the idea of moving back to Sweetheart. Was he crazy to consider uprooting his entire life when Lola hadn't even bothered to tell him she had a doctor's appointment?

Obviously.

Was he fooling himself into hoping they might be able to give this thing between them a second chance? That she'd be able to forgive him and move past what had happened before?

One thing was clear. He needed to take a huge mental step back. At least until he had some answers. "Promise me you won't do anything like this again. I want to know about appointments, when you're not feeling well, names you're thinking about. Anything and everything to do with the baby."

She didn't hesitate. "Absolutely." And her certainty should have made him feel better. But it didn't. Erik couldn't shake the uneasiness that had been building inside him for days, long before this argument.

He was scheduled to leave soon, and he just wasn't sure what he should do—for himself, the baby or Lola.

11

EVER SINCE THE day of her appointment things had been…off. Nothing she could put a finger on, but she could feel more distance between Erik and her than before.

For the past three days they'd done the same things—cooked together, watched TV, slept in the same bed and had explosive sex. They talked about the baby, but never really about the future and how it was going to look.

Lola wasn't sure either of them really knew. But that only increased her anxiety. It was obvious, at least to her, that Erik wasn't making plans to be part of her life because he didn't expect to be.

And meanwhile, she was so in love with him that it hurt. The realization hadn't come as a surprise or even a stark epiphany. It had always been there—never really went away, even when she wished it would. She just hadn't wanted to admit it.

Which only made the way he was drawing away from her hurt that much more. She could feel him slipping through her fingers. And just like before, she was powerless to stop it.

Lola hated feeling powerless.

Deep down, she'd always known that this was how it was going to end, but that didn't make the reality any easier to bear. Erik was going to walk away. She'd fooled herself into thinking she could handle it. That she was stronger now and wouldn't break when he chose his life in California over what they shared.

Although he hadn't told her exactly when he'd be leaving, she knew it was soon. Only a few more days. That was all she had.

The stress of anticipating the fallout was getting to her. Her morning sickness was back with a vengeance and despite the exhaustion, she couldn't sleep. Maybe she should tell him to leave so she could jump straight to the inevitable misery. But she couldn't actually pull the trigger. She wanted to delay the pain as long as possible, but also, something inside her wouldn't let her give up even one minute with him.

Lola was pretty sure that made her pathetic, but she didn't care. Especially when the one place the tension disappeared was in the bedroom. At least there, they were able to connect.

She was desperately trying to find that connection outside the bedroom, too. Tonight she'd made dinner. Nothing fancy, just a roast and some veggies. They'd shared small talk that felt superficial in a way that made Lola's belly ache and turned the food to sawdust in her mouth.

She was in the middle of a sentence, something about

a shoot she'd had that morning, when Erik suddenly pushed his chair back. The legs scraped loudly across the floor, drawing her startled gaze up to his.

"What are you doing?" she asked, carefully setting her fork onto the edge of her plate.

Erik didn't bother to answer. He simply pulled out her chair, gathered her into his arms and headed down the hallway toward her bedroom.

"Oh," she breathed out, wrapping her body tightly around his. Despite the tension filling her, touching him was her only source of relief. When Erik made love to her, she could pretend everything was going to be okay. She could forget what was wrong and allow herself to connect to him on a level that always left her feeling wide open and safe.

Erik nuzzled against her throat, murmuring, "Do you have any idea how beautiful you are? How difficult it is for me to sit across that table from you and keep my hands to myself?"

Despite everything, happiness bubbled up inside her, right along with the need for more of him. Just him.

Lola gripped the edge of his shirt and pulled it out of the way. She found some skin of her own to nuzzle. God, she loved the smell and taste of him. "I can never get enough of you."

"The feeling is mutual."

Reaching her room, Erik didn't even bother turning on a light before spreading her out in the center of the bed. He took his time peeling off her clothes, which was just fine with her. Tonight she was in the mood to savor.

His fingers played over all her sensitive places, coaxing tiny gasps as he flamed her desire higher. He always knew just how to touch her.

This. This was where they spoke the loudest, no matter what else was going on around them.

He worshipped her body, tempting and teasing. Not just with his mouth and fingers, but with his entire body. The power and strength of him as he rubbed against her, chest to chest, thigh to thigh, overwhelmed her.

Her sigh of happiness was soul deep as he finally slipped inside her, joining them in the most primitive and beautiful way possible. He filled her perfectly, stretching and stroking, setting off sparks of heat and pleasure inside her.

Her hands ran across his flanks and back, shoulders and hips, clenching and urging him to go faster. Lola murmured words, soft and sweet, peppered between scorching kisses rained over any inch of skin she could reach.

Her orgasm slammed into her, shocking in its intensity. Lola's entire body thrummed with the overwhelming power of it. His name vibrated across her lips, breathy and tattered, just the way she felt.

Erik's own body contorted as his orgasm crashed right over both of them. She could feel the weight of him pulsing deep inside her and locked her legs around him. She didn't ever want to let go.

Finally, after several minutes, they collapsed to the bed together. Breathless, sweaty and perfect. Limbs tangled together so that she wasn't entirely certain what belonged to whom. Not that it mattered. Everything that was hers was his anyway.

"So good," he whispered, pressing a little kiss to her shoulder even as he tucked her into the shelter of his body.

"So tired," she murmured.

Erik reached down and tugged the covers over them both.

Exhaustion and peace stole over her, dropping her into sleep within seconds.

But that peace was shaken several hours later when a rhythmic pounding jolted her from sleep. Disoriented, at first Lola thought the noise was coming from somewhere in her bedroom. But sitting straight up, she realized Erik was already yanking on a pair of jeans and heading for the hallway.

Someone was at her front door. Glancing at the bedside clock, she realized it was after midnight. This was not going to be good.

Bleary-eyed, Lola threw on a short silk robe and padded down the hallway behind him.

Peering over his shoulder, she discovered the last person she'd expected to see—her father.

Memories of another knock on another night swamped her. Colt's accident, her mother's death. Lola's knees buckled, but somehow she caught herself on the doorframe, letting it hold her up.

A sense of doom and disaster washed over her. Familiar and so frightening. She started to shake her head, deny whatever was happening.

But she, better than most, understood denial couldn't stop fate, cruel bitch that she was, from taking what she wanted.

AFTER YEARS OF being programmed to wake from a dead sleep to respond, Erik was wide awake when he opened Lola's door.

"Sir," he said, ushering Lola's father in even as his heart rate picked up speed.

Nothing good could come from this.

Chief Whittaker's expression was hard and unhappy. It didn't help when the other man pushed past him just in time to grab Lola and guide her over to the couch. Her face was pale, her gorgeous brown eyes saucer-wide and full of pain.

Erik hadn't realized she'd followed him.

He watched as her dad crouched in front of her, speaking in a soothing voice. "Everyone's fine, baby."

Lola sucked in a harsh breath. She nodded and murmured, "Okay."

Patting her hand, chief stood and turned to take Erik in.

It was hardly the first time he'd spoken to Keith since he'd been back. In fact, they'd had multiple conversations, but all of them had been centered around work. Business, not the easy father/son relationship they'd shared for years.

Keith's opinion mattered so much to Erik, and given everything that had happened, it was difficult to look him in the eye. More so than Colt or Lola, even.

"I'm sorry to stop by so late. I tried to call, but you didn't answer. I just received a call from the fire chief in Marin."

"Okay," Erik pulled the single word out, trepidation and anxiety crackling across his skin.

"Some idiot walked away from a campfire yesterday morning without making sure it was out. With the dry summer and high temps we've been having, they've got an out-of-control wildfire on their hands and have requested assistance."

And of course Lola's dad would send men. "Who's going?"

"I can spare a handful of guys. They'll be heading out in a couple hours. But when I told Chief you were in town and had specialized experience as a smoke jumper, he asked if I could talk you into coming, too."

Of course he would go. There was no hesitation or decision to be made. Fighting wildfires was everyday for him. Something he was trained to handle. "I'll grab my gear and meet the rest of the guys. At the station?"

"Yeah." Chief hesitated long enough that the last cobwebs cleared out of Erik's brain.

Crossing the room, Keith laid a hand on his shoulder and squeezed. The men were roughly the same height, but that did nothing to extinguish the sensation that Erik was looking up at someone much wiser and more honorable than he could ever hope to be.

"Do me a favor, son."

God, it had been a long time since he'd heard Chief call him *son.* "Anything."

"Be careful. This fire is…nasty. It's eating acres like a hungry beast with Marin right in its path. And I know you. You're the kind of man who will put his own life on the line if it means saving someone else's. Which is admirable. But you're not invincible."

Erik felt the dig deep into his soul, the reminder that he wasn't perfect and had cost this man's son so much.

Apparently his face telegraphed every stricken thought that crossed his brain, because suddenly the pressure on his shoulder was so intense it rivaled the pain lancing through his chest.

"That's not what I meant, Erik. We've never talked about that night. Not really. I know you think I blame you, but I don't. Colt made his own decisions. Yes, as your chief I was pissed—still am—at both of you for disobeying a direct order. As your father—and I'm just as much yours as his—I admired you both for risking so much to save someone else.

"Life is rarely easy or cut and dried. Everything about that night is twisted for all of us. But that doesn't mean I don't love you and care about you just as much, because I do. And I don't want to see you get hurt. Not just for yourself, but for my daughter and the baby you have on the way now."

Erik sucked in a heavy breath, the sound ricocheting through the room and rattling deep inside his chest. A pressure that had been there so long he'd stopped noticing it finally eased.

"Just…think about the people who love you before you do anything rash. That's all I'm asking, okay?"

"Okay," Erik answered, his voice gruff.

Crossing the room, Chief laid a kiss on Lola's forehead, said, "I'll tell them you're on your way," and then walked out the door.

Erik stared at Lola, blinking for several seconds and trying to get his head to stop whirling. How could five minutes change so much? With a few simple words and an absolution he'd craved but never thought he deserved, Keith had just blown apart the guilt and fear that had been driving Erik for so long.

Pushing up from the couch, Lola crossed the room, her gaze steady and sure on his the entire time. Pressing her forehead to his chest, she wrapped her arms around him and squeezed. He could feel the tension in her body. Recognized that he should do something to ease it, but there was nothing to say.

His job was dangerous and she'd always known it.

Finally she pulled back, poised and composed as only Lola could be, which was exactly what he needed right now. "Let me help. What do you need?"

Erik pulled her up onto her toes and found her lips, delving in to take the sweet heat that she wordlessly offered.

"I need you to get back into bed and get some sleep. I'll call when I can."

GET SOME SLEEP. Yeah, right. She knew he needed her to at least pretend, so Lola had climbed into bed and listened as Erik rustled around her house, quickly grabbing what he needed before heading out. But she hadn't slept.

And for the last two days, since he'd left, her heart had been permanently lodged in her throat. Her cell had become attached to her hand because she knew the crazy hours he had to be working and feared missing any call from him. He hadn't called. After the first day, she'd convinced herself he was just busy. The information coming in on the news was bad, and the updates her dad had given her were even more grim.

Marin was surrounded by forest on two sides, and the fire was spreading toward it. Rain wasn't in the forecast for several days. Their only real hope had been a shift in the winds, although that just meant someone else would fall into the fire's path.

South Carolina wasn't known for major forest fires, but there had been a perfect storm of events leading to this one burning out of control. The story had hit the national news, and the governor had requested help from states with more experienced teams.

The longer her phone was silent, the more her fear raged unchecked. And the less she expected a call from Erik and started expecting a call from someone else telling her he'd been injured or worse.

The nightmare she'd pushed down for so long reared up, overtaking every thought in her brain. For years she'd lived with the dread and constant tension every time her dad—her only living parent—put himself in danger to protect others.

The job was noble, but Lola couldn't silence the voice in her head that wanted to beg her dad to quit. But then she felt guilty for being weak and selfish.

The relief when her father had stopped fighting fires and taken the position as Chief was short-lived as Colt and Erik followed in his footsteps. And every horror she'd imagined had come to life the night of Colt's accident.

Colt's injuries were too big a price to pay, but being

able to live without the stress and fear these last few years had been her silver lining.

Until now.

Lola was trying to fill her time as much as possible with work, the best way she could think to get through the days. Her body was exhausted, but her mind wouldn't let her rest.

Colt had already fussed at her for pushing herself too hard, not that it had helped. He was currently mumbling to himself, irritated as hell, as he rolled around the studio, cleaning up from her last session.

Normally Lola would have helped him. But Colt wasn't the only one who was irritated, and she figured it was better for them both to have a little space. Besides, her back was sore and she really just wanted to sit down. Not to mention pee. She'd needed to since the middle of her session, but the toddler she'd been working with had been difficult, and she hadn't wanted to leave once they got her settled and engaged with the camera.

Maybe Lola would indulge in a little nap. Get Colt off her back if nothing else.

Then Lola looked down and noticed a streak of red across her thigh.

Her heart leaped into her chest, and every speck of blood drained out of her head. Reaching out for something to hold on to as dizziness overtook her, she started to yell for Erik before remembering that he wasn't there.

A sense of stark isolation overwhelmed her. God, she needed him. So much. But she hadn't heard from him since he took off.

She couldn't handle this right now. No, panic wasn't an option.

Taking a deep breath, Lola forced herself to stop and think. She was strong enough to deal with whatever happened. And she wasn't alone, no matter how much it felt that way.

Coming out of the bathroom, she snagged her phone before walking into the front studio. "Colt, I need you to take me to my doctor's office."

She was already speaking to the nurse before her brother could answer. With a calm she was far from feeling, Lola relayed what was going on. As she'd expected, they wanted her to come in right away. Colt, listening to her end of the conversation, was already headed out to his specially equipped truck.

Lola grabbed her purse, called Hope and asked her friend to meet her. Hope had experienced something similar when she was pregnant with the twins, and right now Lola needed a voice of reason to keep her steady.

She wasn't at the doctor's office five minutes before Hope, Lexi, Willow and Tatum all came barreling in. They spoke over each other, surrounding her. Colt quietly backed away, letting the women take over.

Hope sat beside her and grasped her hand. "Everything's going to be fine, Lola."

Just hearing the reassurance that she'd needed so much the minute she saw blood had her head throbbing again. She swallowed and nodded, even though there was a part of her that didn't believe.

Couldn't believe.

Of course she was losing Erik's baby. She'd wanted it

too much, and she was being punished. With the baby, even if she couldn't have Erik, she'd have a piece of him. It was a realization she hadn't admitted even to herself.

But fate didn't want her to have anyone. She'd lost her mother and Erik, and she'd come damn close to losing Colt. Lived with the possibility of losing her father for years.

The one thing she'd thought would be safe—wholly hers and absolutely protected—was this baby.

A few minutes later, the nurse ushered her into an examination room. Hope went with her.

It should have been Erik, but it wasn't, and no amount of wishing would change that.

Somewhere in between the questions and the ultrasound that showed a strong, healthy heartbeat, resolve quickened deep inside her.

According to the doctor, her baby was okay. He couldn't tell her what had caused the bleeding but assured her that during the first trimester it wasn't uncommon. They'd keep a closer eye on her and the baby over the next few weeks, but he admonished her to slow down and de-stress.

Something Colt was all too happy to echo when Hope relayed the doctor's instructions to everyone in the waiting room. Great, now she'd have half the town trying to get her to take it easy for the next seven months.

As she walked out of the clinic, she took stock of the people who had been there when she'd needed them.

Maybe it wasn't fair, because it wasn't like Erik had simply flaked and not shown up, but his absence was glaringly painful. She hadn't even called him, and had extracted a promise from all of them that they wouldn't, either. No matter what was happening to her, Erik was in the middle of fighting a dangerous fire, and the last thing he needed was a distraction.

But the result was still the same. Once again, he wasn't present when she'd needed him. He'd extended his stay to fight the fire in Marin, but when it was over he'd go home to California and she'd be alone for good. Sure, he said he wanted to be involved, and she honestly believed he meant it.

In reality, he'd be on the other side of the country. He couldn't be here for her, and it was time Lola stopped pretending otherwise. She hadn't wanted to deal with the truth, but now it was time. Seeing the flutter of her baby's heartbeat on that monitor had hammered home one thing in particular.

She was everything to that baby, and he or she deserved for her to be strong and do the right thing for all of them.

12

ONCE SHE WAS settled at home, Lola sent everyone away. Curling up on her sofa had been heavenly, and all of the emotional turmoil had caused her to fall asleep almost as soon as her eyes closed. But for the second time in a few days, a loud bang on the front door startled her.

Lola jerked up, her heart lurching uncomfortably inside her chest. Rubbing at her gritty eyes, she was still half-asleep when she opened the door to find Hope and Willow standing on her front porch.

Dusk was just starting to creep across the sky behind them, so it wasn't late enough for her automatically to think something was wrong. Considering her scare today, it was possible they were just here to check on her.

Except for their matching grim expressions.

"What's wrong?" Lola asked.

Hope and Willow shared a pointed look, but didn't answer. Instead, Hope asked, "How are you feeling? Any more bleeding or cramping?"

"I'm fine. Will you both just quit it and tell me what the hell is going on?"

The two of them shared another glance. Then Hope moved a little closer and said, "There are reports that several of the firefighters working outside Marin were cut off from the team and trapped."

"They're working on getting them rescued," Willow rushed to add, "but the news is saying a couple of them are severely injured. They're not reporting who."

Lola swayed. Willow reached for her, drawing her in. "At least one of the guys is ours."

"Have you heard from Erik?" Hope asked softly. "Did you call him after you left the doctor's office?"

"No," she whispered. "I haven't heard from him since he left."

It was all too much. Everything. Lola's body went cold. She felt herself shutting down, knew the signs because she'd gone through it before—with her mother, with Colt.

Her emotions switched off so that she could deal with the potential tragedy in front of her with that calm control that Erik seemed to value so much.

She hadn't even realized Willow was still grasping her arm until she and Hope steered her over to the couch and gently pushed her down. Her gaze landed on her cell on the coffee table. Without thinking, she picked it up and called him, something she hadn't let herself do in the two days he'd been gone.

It went straight to voice mail.

What the hell did that mean? Was his phone a melted mess because it had gotten burned up in the fire? Or had he been too busy to charge it and now it was dead?

The edges of her phone bit into Lola's palm as she punched in another number. Her father's gruff voice, normally so soothing, sent a spurt of despair shooting through the cold trying to engulf her. "Dad. I just heard. Who?"

"Baby," her dad rumbled. "I don't know yet."

Lola shook her head, logically knowing he couldn't see her response but unable to do anything else.

"I'll let you know as soon as I hear more. But...baby, he's good and smart. I'm sure he's fine."

"You don't know that," she whispered. "Even good and smart guys get hurt." Neither one of them needed to say her brother's name to know exactly what she meant.

She hung up, knowing there was nothing else her dad could say right now that would help. Hours ago she'd resolved to end things with Erik. To put the baby's needs first and save herself some inevitable heartache.

And here she was, experiencing that heartache anyway.

She couldn't keep doing this. Her entire relationship with Erik since he'd returned had been a roller-coaster ride that left her breathless from the highs and aching from the lows.

She'd lost too many people. Experienced too much tragedy and too many close calls to continue tempting fate.

Nope, she was through.

FIRE BURNED ALL around him. His skin felt like it was going to bubble up and melt off his body. The heat was unbearable, but he pressed forward anyway. He didn't have a choice.

Somewhere, lost in the haze of smoke and licking flames, was a cluster of men he'd sent straight into hell.

Men he knew and had fought beside. Men whose kids he'd held and wives he'd teased.

Everything about this situation felt like déjà vu. Two months ago he'd buried a friend, a man he'd come to trust and respect. He couldn't take doing that again.

The restless, desperate edge that had ridden him after Aaron's death was back and bigger than ever. The same recklessness that had gotten him put on administrative leave for two months in the first place.

Not that it mattered. Not when lives were on the line.

There was no way he could look Caroline or Dani in the eye and tell them their husbands were dead because he'd fucked up.

Guilt, so strong and goddamn familiar, ate at his gut like battery acid. It pushed him forward when every cell in his body was urging him to retreat.

"Slow down, Erik," one of the other guys hollered over the crackle of the flames devouring the towering trees around them.

A hard hand grabbed him, jerking him to a halt. Frustration flared through him. Yanking out of the grasp, he spun to lash out with words, but had to swallow them when he realized the man who'd stopped him was the chief of Marin's fire department.

"The last thing we need is to have more men cut off. Erik, I get it. I want to find them, too. And we will. The best way to do that is to keep our heads."

Logically, Erik knew the other man was right. But instinct told him if they didn't hurry there'd be nothing left to find except ashes. And he refused to let that happen.

Not when he was the one who'd sent the men out here in the first place. Because of his experience, Chief had placed him on point for determining the safest place for the men to be deployed. His brain told him no one could have anticipated the sudden shift in wind, not even the meteorologists he'd consulted. But that didn't stop the terror building steadily inside him.

"I hear you," he said, rubbing his hands roughly through his hair. Grit and soot covered every inch of his body, and exhaustion pulled at him like a boulder whenever he stopped.

So he couldn't stop.

He couldn't remember the last time he'd eaten or slept. The fire didn't sleep, so neither could he. Not if he wanted to win.

Together, his team clustered and discussed the direction they needed to head in. Other teams were fanning out within a one-mile radius, searching. They were all working off the last radio transmission the lost team had sent, telling them the fire had shifted and they were surrounded by flames with no way out. They didn't even have their full gear since they'd been sent to cut down a firebreak, not fight the actual fire.

Erik kept his mouth shut and impatiently listened, ready for action, not discussion. Regrouped, his team headed back out, yelling and looking for any sign of movement. It was late, the middle of the night, when Erik heard the faintest voice raised above the grumble of fire.

Sending up a cry of his own, he raced toward the sound and slammed right into a wall of heat. The sensation of it reverberated through his body, making his teeth clack together in surprise and pain.

But he kept moving forward, alternating yelling and waiting in silence for an answer. The responses got louder, giving him hope where there'd been little an hour before.

"Please, God," he murmured.

Five minutes later he broke through a stand of trees and into a clearing that was consumed by hip-high flames. On the other side of that wall of fire, he could make out the hazy outline of three men. There should have been five.

Erik charged forward, moved to the left and then ran to the right, looking for a break in the flames so that he could reach the men. The hope he'd allowed to flare a few moments ago morphed into dread, but he shook himself. He'd find a way out of this. He had to.

Getting as close as he could, Erik hollered to the men on the other side. "I don't see a way in to you. Can you move in either direction?"

Maybe they could find an opening further down.

"Erik!" one of the men hollered. Squinting, he realized the voice was familiar, belonged to Nick, one of the guys from Sweetheart. Relief gushed through him, warm and hopeful before he realized that Brian, the other firefighter from their team, wasn't standing beside him.

"No," Nick answered. "Brian and one of the other

guys are injured. We've been carrying them for several miles, but they need medical attention now."

There was no hiding the desperation in Nick's voice. *Shit.* No. He wasn't ready to watch another one of his brothers carried away from a fire on a stretcher, his life forever changed because of a decision Erik had made.

Beside him, the other guys from his search team poured into the clearing. Chief jogged up beside them, leaning over with his hands on his knees to catch his breath. Looking up at Erik, he said, "Now what?"

Every pair of eyes turned to him, waiting for orders. He was the one with the experience and training to handle this situation. Erik felt a tremor of fear rocking his body but pushed it back. Refused to let it take hold.

At least not until they had those men safe.

"Two of the men are injured and need medical assistance. They can't travel anymore. I can't find a break in the flames, which means we're going to have to go through them."

The men around him shared grim looks, but no one argued.

The firefighters took up positions within the team without further discussion. They hadn't worked together and the roles weren't rehearsed, but that didn't matter.

Checking his own protective gear, Erik took a deep breath, picked the spot with the lowest flames and ran full-tilt toward them. The sensation was difficult to describe, fire surrounding his entire body for moments that felt so long but probably took only a few heartbeats.

A few seconds later, another member of the group followed him. Together, they transported the injured men, one suffering from burns and the other from a potential broken ankle, across the flames. Twenty minutes after Erik had found them, all five missing firefighters were safe.

Medflight had been called to pick up the injured men as Erik had worked to rescue the others, so he had no idea how Brian was.

Sweat and soot mixed on his skin. As soon as it was safe, Erik ripped his gear off. Despite the heavy weight of smoke still clogging the air, for the first time in hours he felt like he could breathe.

He tugged his soaked shirt over his head and used it to wipe grime from his face. Pure adrenaline was still pumping into his system, but he knew it would disappear soon enough and he'd probably crash. In the meantime, he needed to find out about Brian.

Walking across to the cluster of men standing at the edge of the clearing, Erik was intent on asking, but didn't get a chance. From behind, someone snagged his arm and spun him.

"Erik, you're hurt."

He turned to find Chief gingerly gripping his left arm, holding it up and out. His answer was automatic. "No, I'm not." But the minute the words escaped his mouth, the pain hit, hot and hard.

It stole his breath, ripping up his arm and across his chest in a throbbing path. Jerking his gaze down, Erik was stunned to see red, angry streaks running across the back of his left hand and up his wrist and forearm. When had he gotten burned?

"How did that happen?" he asked. He'd been wearing his protective gear. No, wait. Frustrated because he couldn't get the gear onto Brian, he'd ripped off his own gloves and hadn't put them back on. "Shit, I didn't even feel it."

Chief didn't bother responding, instead grabbing the radio attached to his shoulder and calling for an ambulance. Any other day, Erik might have argued, but considering everything that had happened in the last forty-eight hours and the pain tearing through his gut, he decided medical attention was his best option.

At least in the back of an ambulance he couldn't fuck up and get anyone else hurt.

THE LAST FEW hours had been a whirlwind, fighting his own doctors while he tried to find out Brian's and the other firefighter's condition. Erik allowed his burns to be treated only after he heard the news: Brian's broken ankle required surgery but he was doing well, and the other man had mostly second-degree burns and would recover.

Erik had been lucky, as well. The burns on his hand and arm were first-degree, even though they were severe enough to blister badly. He'd need to keep them clean and bandaged, but they would heal within a few weeks.

He'd be out of commission for a while, though, so when he was released, he was told to go straight home. The first thing he wanted to do was call Lola, but it was so late that he was afraid he'd wake her.

Instead, he drove straight to her place and found every light in the house blazing, Lola asleep on the sofa.

Normally he'd have gently gathered her into his arms and carried her back to bed, but with his hand wrapped in about half a roll of gauze, that wasn't really an option. Especially when right about now he was regretting his refusal to take painkillers at the hospital. His whole arm throbbed, sore and hot.

Still, he wasn't about to let her spend all night on the couch.

Kneeling beside her, Erik let his uninjured fingers slip across her forehead and down her cheek. "Lola," he murmured. "Baby, wake up."

She whimpered and stirred. Her arms tightened around her middle as he continued to stroke her face. "Lo," he tried again.

Slowly her eyes fluttered open. They were deep and sad, which made a knot the size of a fist form in his belly.

"Baby, what's wrong?"

"Erik." The sharp pink tip of her tongue snuck out, sweeping across her parted lips. At least he wasn't in so much pain that he couldn't notice—and respond—to the little things. Now his hand wasn't the only thing throbbing.

And suddenly, the idea of burying himself deep inside her, wrapping himself in the sweet heat of Lola, was the only remedy he wanted.

Erik dragged his thumb across her slick bottom lip, but her response wasn't what he'd expected. Instead of leaning into his caress, she pulled away, breaking the contact.

She sat up, using her hands to sweep her cloud of hair away from her face.

"You're okay," she said.

"Of course I am."

Her gaze darted over his body, cataloging everything in a split second. "What happened to your hand?"

"Burns, first-degree. I had to get to some of our guys who were in trouble. Everyone's fine. Brian broke his ankle, but he's already out of surgery and should be good as new in a couple months. Another guy has second-degree burns across his torso and leg, but it could be worse. They don't think grafts will be necessary. He'll recover."

She nodded, her expression shuttered. Something twisted in his gut.

"Why didn't you call me?" she asked.

"Everything happened so fast." He reached for a lock of hair and tried to tuck it behind her ear, but she jerked out of his grasp.

No, not good.

"They whisked me away in an ambulance," he explained, "took my clothes, my phone, everything."

"And you couldn't ask a nurse to call me?"

"I didn't think about it. I just wanted to get treated and released. Besides, it's the middle of the night. I thought you'd be asleep and didn't want to wake you."

Lola pushed up from the sofa and brushed past him, her body stiff with tension. Spinning on her heel, she pinned him with a look.

Her voice was even and low, firm, as she said, "I'm glad you're okay, but I think you should go."

"What?" Erik took a step toward her.

But Lola held out her hands. "Don't."

"Lola, what's going on?"

"Nothing. Nothing except me coming to my senses and realizing that this has no future. I can't do this anymore, Erik. I can't risk putting everything I have into you when you're never going to be willing to do the same for me."

Erik shook his head, bewildered. "I don't understand."

"And that's part of the problem. Hope and Willow came to tell me what was going on tonight. I talked to my dad. Several of the firefighters' wives called to check on me. But you, you didn't bother. I worried about you all night, Erik. For the last two days, actually."

The accusation in her voice cut deep. "I'm sorr—"

"That's not going to fix this. For the last seven hours I've lived with the possibility that you might be gone." Fear sparked in the back of her gaze, finally pushing against the blank darkness.

"I'm right here, baby."

"For how long? You're going to leave. I've always known that. For someone who grew up hoping to be anyone but his father, you've definitely gotten the whole running away thing down."

Her words sliced through him, hurting a hell of a lot worse than his injuries ever could.

"The bottom line is, I can't count on you. I never could. The baby and I don't need you here, Erik. Go home to California."

Everything she said played into his worst fears and

deepest anxieties. She was right. She couldn't count on him because he always screwed up. Just like tonight when he'd sent those men straight into danger. Just like with Colt.

She wasn't wrong, and her words dredged up the one idea he couldn't quite banish—he didn't deserve her or the happiness she gave him.

And Lola had finally figured it out.

13

LOLA HADN'T EXPECTED Erik's resigned acceptance and quiet exit from her life—again. He hadn't fought or argued. Had barely looked at her as he'd nodded and walked out her door.

And that was it. Her world crushed, a second time.

She'd gotten so little sleep lately that she basically spent twenty-four hours in bed. Once her friends, brother and dad learned about her fight with Erik they all stopped by to check on her, but she communicated little aside from assuring them that she was healthy and just needed some time.

She wasn't ready to talk about it.

The next day she forced herself out of bed and back into her normal routine. She was the one who'd made the decision to end things. Lola was pretty sure wallowing wasn't allowed in that situation. At least, not for long.

Part of her was waiting—for Erik to show up and argue with her. For him to fight for their relationship.

For him to reassure her that he really was in this for the long haul.

Instead, she found out from Colt that he'd gone back to California.

And in that moment, any hope she'd been harboring withered and died. In its place bloomed the realization that she'd pushed him away. Erik had left her once, deciding what they had wasn't enough. So she'd forced him to that point again, hoping he'd choose her this time.

He hadn't.

His actions reinforced what she'd already known. They could never have worked. Yes, she was still going to have to figure out how to coparent with him. They had a few months before they'd deal with that. A few months for her to lick her wounds, heal her shattered heart and figure out how to put her child's needs above her own.

A few months—not something she needed to tackle today.

Today, and probably for the next few weeks, Lola decided she was perfectly within her rights to be grumpy and miserable.

"God, you two are a pair," Colt grumbled.

"What?" Lola asked, jerking her gaze up from the computer screen she'd been staring blindly at for heaven only knew how long.

"Erik came by yesterday wearing pretty much the exact same expression. I've never met two people more perfect for each other so hell-bent on screwing everything up."

"We're not perfect for each other." The last few days proved that.

"Bullshit. I've watched you both for years, Lola. Trust me when I say you're perfect together. You bring out the best in Erik, remind him that life isn't always serious and heavy. It isn't all responsibility or making up for his father's shortcomings. And he does the same for you, forces you to slow down and appreciate what you've worked so hard to achieve. He draws out that gorgeous smile no one gets to see nearly enough. He forces you out from behind the lens and into the action."

Lola sucked in a harsh breath. He did do that for her. Tears clogged her throat, thickening her words. "He left."

"According to him it was because you didn't give him any choice."

She shook her head. "He could have refused. Could have fought."

Colt raised a single eyebrow. "Because you were in the frame of mind to listen?"

No, she hadn't been. She'd been so wrapped up in her own anger, doubt and misery that she wouldn't have heard much of anything. But he'd more than just left her house. He'd left the damn state.

"Did you even tell him about your scare with the baby?"

Lola didn't answer, which was pretty much answer enough.

"That's what I thought. You can't punish him for something he didn't even know was happening, Lo."

"But he wasn't there!" she hollered, then gasped. She wasn't talking about a few days ago.

God, she was so messed up. "He wasn't there," she murmured again, because even realizing she was still holding on to her hurt and pain from before didn't make it go away.

Slowly Colt rolled over to her. He placed his fingers beneath her chin and forced her to look at him. "I know, but you're going to have to forgive him."

She'd thought she had. Really. But apparently she'd just hoped that eventually she could.

"I don't know how," she whispered. "How did you?"

Colt shrugged. "It took me a while to shoulder the blame for my own actions, Lo. But once I did, forgiving him for everything that came afterward was just a matter of seeing things from his perspective."

"You make it sound so damn easy."

He laughed. "Trust me, it's not. It's the hardest thing I've ever done, but I needed to do it for me. I needed to do it for him. Because I knew one day he'd be back and he'd need me to look him in the eye and tell him it was okay. To reassure him that I could see him clearly, as the brother he's always been."

Tears clogged Lola's throat, scratchy and choking.

"You love him, Lo."

"Of course I do." She could feel her heart trembling, throbbing with the pain of her reality. "But sometimes love isn't enough. We just can't seem to get it right, and I'm tired of being the one to end up hurt."

A sad expression crossed his face. "I'm going to tell you what I told him. Sometimes love doesn't last or work, or the people we care about leave or die. But that doesn't mean you walk away from the possibility of it when you have the chance to try. Especially when the only thing holding you back is fear."

THE LAST TWO days had been a blur. With nothing to keep him in Sweetheart, Erik had done exactly what Lola had told him to do. He'd left.

This time, leaving had hurt so much worse. Six years ago he'd been running from guilt and fear. This time, those fears had come to life when Lola had looked at him with that frozen expression and told him he was just like his father.

She wasn't wrong.

Standing on the balcony of his apartment, staring up at the clear blue sky, Erik realized that California wasn't home anymore, if it ever had been. None of the places he'd lived since leaving Sweetheart had been, so he'd never stayed long.

Hell, even looking around his place, it was clear he'd barely taken the time to make it livable. The furniture was sparse and functional. There was only a handful of photographs, mostly of his mother, except for one blown up and framed above his sofa.

He loved that beach scene Lola had photographed on a family vacation to the coast when she was eighteen. It was the one constant no matter where he went.

Even his job...he'd been away for two months now and barely missed it. Before he would have sworn that he was addicted to the adrenaline rush and the way fighting wildfires made him feel alive.

But that had been a half truth, too. Yes, there were aspects of it he'd miss, but being a smoke jumper wasn't the only thing that made him feel alive.

Touching Lola had always given him the same rush. The way she'd looked at him—back then and now—with admiration and acceptance in her gaze...that was true addiction. He wanted that every day of his life.

He'd gone to see Colt before he'd left. The least he could do was tell him goodbye this time. But that conversation hadn't gone nearly as expected.

Colt had been pissed, not just because he'd hurt Lola, but because he was running away. Again. Hurting them both.

At first, Erik had let Colt yell at him. He'd deserved it. Right up until he'd used his chair to literally back Erik into a corner, berating him to the point that he'd finally fought back, screaming that Lola was better off without him.

Just saying those words out loud had changed everything.

Colt scoffed at his deepest fear, dismissing it out of hand and logically picking apart every argument he'd thrown at him for why he didn't deserve to be happy.

Hours later, it was clear that Colt was going to make a wonderful therapist because Erik's entire world had been turned upside down by the things Colt had made him admit and see.

And he'd finally laid some of the fears that had driven him away to rest.

But not all of them.

He knew Lola was angry with him, for things he'd

done now and things he'd done then. She might never be able to forgive him, and that thought scared the shit out of him.

But Colt was right. He couldn't let fear rule his life anymore. It was time to grow up and become the man—the father—he'd always wanted to be.

The man Lola had seen in him, the man she and their child deserved.

And that started with making a leap of faith and hoping hard work and genuine honesty would be enough to win her back. Because despite all of the mistakes, they both deserved to be happy. And he now believed he could give that to her.

At a knock on his door, Erik turned away from the view for the last time.

Opening the door, he let Wes, his closest friend here, inside. "Hey, man. Thanks for your help."

"Anytime, although on the drive over here I did have an argument with myself about whether I was going to try to talk you out of this."

"You can try, but it won't work."

Wes sighed. "I always knew you were temporary, anyway."

It was really starting to bother Erik that everyone in his life seemed to think that.

"Even if your reputation hadn't preceded you, the first time all the guys went out for beers after work solidified it. I knew there was someone who had a hold on you and figured eventually she'd come back around. Just tell me one thing. Are you happy?"

Erik fought back a rusty laugh. "Not yet, but I think maybe I could be. She's pregnant."

Wes whistled. "Well, don't you move fast."

Not nearly fast enough. It had taken him six long years to get up the courage to make amends. He wasn't willing to wait even six days this time.

"The movers will be here tomorrow to pack everything. Just…" Erik let his gaze rake across his apartment. "Honestly, the only thing I really care about is that photograph on the wall. Don't let them screw it up."

Wes gave him a crooked smile. "You bet. But I'll make sure they don't scratch the furniture, either. They know where to deliver everything?"

This was where he'd taken that huge leap of faith, because as far as he was concerned, failure wasn't an option.

"Yep." He'd given the movers Lola's address. He figured it would take them about a week to drive his stuff across the country. By then he'd have convinced her that he was serious, or she'd see the moving van with all his stuff pull into her driveway, and that would do the convincing for him.

Worst case scenario, she'd burn everything. But, like he'd said, the only thing he really cared about was that photograph.

Erik slapped the key to his place into Wes's hand.

Aside from Colt, Wes was his closest friend. It was difficult to say goodbye knowing he was leaving for the other side of the country.

Erik reached for the other man, slapping his back

and pulling him in for a quick hug. "Going to miss you, man."

Wes just laughed. "You think you're getting rid of me that easy? You know I wanna meet your girl. Maddie, the triplets and I expect an invitation to visit soon."

THE NEXT MORNING, Colt's words were still ringing through Lola's head. Not just their conversation yesterday, but the one before when he'd explained just how they'd failed Erik. She'd tossed and turned all night, and somewhere around 2:00 a.m. had come to a decision.

She was a coward.

That was the long and short of it. And considering how much she'd prided herself on being just as strong as the men around her, able to handle any crisis with calm and conviction…the realization was a slap to the face.

Yes, she'd been pissed at Erik because he'd also taken the cowardly approach to dealing with what had happened to Colt. He'd run away from his own guilt, using the excuse that other people would believe the worst in him. When really, he'd done what he'd thought was kindest to the people who mattered most.

He'd wanted to save her father and Colt the pain of telling him he wasn't good enough. By avoiding them, he'd live with his own worst fears—that he didn't deserve to be happy and loved, something he'd been afraid of since his father left.

But here she was, doing the same damn thing and blaming him for that, too.

She loved Erik, but she'd abandoned him to his own vulnerability and reinforced the lies that his father's actions had taught him. She needed to convince him that he was worthy of being loved and wanted.

So at 4:00 a.m. she'd started packing her bags, gone online and bought a plane ticket to California. She didn't have his address, but she was pretty certain she could get it. And that was a bridge she'd cross when she needed to.

In the meantime, she had several hours to kill before she had to be at the airport in Charleston. She'd already called Colt and asked him to handle the logistics at the studio. She'd told her dad where she was going and why.

With two hours left before she needed to leave for the airport, Lola heard a car pull into her driveway.

She half expected to see Colt's truck as she glanced out the window, but instead found a silver SUV she didn't recognize.

She was even more puzzled when the driver's door opened and Erik got out.

Without thinking, Lola yanked open her front door. "Erik?"

His gaze jerked up, hope and light singeing her. "Lola."

The way he breathed her name, like saying it was the only thing keeping him alive, suddenly smoothed the tangle of emotions she'd been fighting for days, melting the pain away.

He was here and that was all that mattered.

"What are you doing? I thought you were in California."

Erik's mouth twisted. "I was, but only to pack up

my things. Lola, my life isn't there anymore. I'm not sure it ever was."

She drew in a halting breath, a hiccup following. Hearing those words…they meant everything to her.

Lola crossed the porch and stopped at the top of the steps. "Erik, I'm so sorry."

"What do you have to apologize for? I'm the one who broke your heart. I'm the one who betrayed your trust in me."

"Maybe, but I'm the one who's been making you pay for something that wasn't your fault. I told you it was fine, that I didn't blame you. But deep down, I still did."

Pain crossed Erik's face. He strode across her front lawn, stopping at the bottom of her stairs and looking up. "Do you now?"

Did she? Lola stared at him. Really looked deep. Because before she answered, she needed to be absolutely certain she was telling him the truth. Erik deserved no less.

At her hesitation, he said, "Whatever your answer is, we'll deal with it together."

And that certainty more than anything else destroyed any vestiges of blame and grief she might have been hanging on to.

"No, Erik. I don't blame you for Colt's accident. I forgive you for leaving when things got rough. Can you forgive me for not going after you? I let my own fears and emotions get in the way of proving to you that my love was strong enough for both of us when you needed it."

Lola held her breath, hoping and waiting. There was

no doubt in her mind that Erik loved her as much as she loved him. What she needed to know this time around was that they were both in it for the long haul.

They'd fight and have disagreements. There'd definitely come a day when they'd both have to beat back their own demons. But they each needed to trust that the other would stand and fight instead of giving in.

A crooked smile curled Erik's lips right before he bounded onto her front porch and pulled her tight against him.

It would have been so easy just to melt into his embrace. To let herself take the strength and safety he was offering.

But first she needed to be completely honest with him.

"The fire wasn't the only thing that scared me, Erik. That afternoon I started bleeding."

Pushing her back, Erik's hands had a death grip on her arms. "You didn't tell me." His words were accusing, and she deserved every ounce of it.

"No, and I'm sorry. I was scared and angry because you weren't there." She pressed her palms to his chest, hating herself a little for the speed of his heart. "Yes, I know that wasn't fair. The baby is fine. I would have told you immediately if it wasn't, no matter what else had happened. But I needed to tell you now."

For several seconds, Erik stared down at her, clearly unhappy. Lola held her breath, expecting a lecture she absolutely deserved. She'd made him a promise that she wouldn't shut him out of anything that happened with the baby and then, at the first sign of trouble, had done just that.

"From now on, you'll be the first to know everything. I promise."

Closing his eyes, Erik pulled in a deep breath and then let it go again. "God, we're a pair, aren't we?"

Relief swept through her. Her voice a little shaky, Lola admitted, "Yeah, but eventually we're going to get it right. I love you, Erik, and have since long before you gave me that beautiful new camera."

Leaning in, Erik found her mouth. The kiss was all heat and power, a reminder of just what they'd always shared. And within minutes, Lola was breathless and wanting more.

But Erik didn't give it to her. Instead he pulled back and swiped a soft hand across her forehead. "I've loved you for years, Lola, and I'll love you until my last day."

Epilogue

THE CHAOS AROUND them should have left Lola exhausted, but instead she was energized. Which, considering she had a six-week-old baby and sleep was at a premium, was a miracle.

They'd gathered together for a belated baby shower, since Miss Lily Grace had decided to arrive four weeks early. Those first few weeks had been difficult, since the little one had spent nineteen days in the NICU. But everything about their baby girl was perfect.

Erik still struggled now and again with worrying he might break her. She'd been so tiny when she'd arrived, her skin so thin they could practically see the blood pumping through the blue veins underneath.

Lola didn't like to remember those days—or nights—but the one bright spot in the whole experience had been Erik by her side. He'd been her rock, promising her that everything would be fine no matter what.

And he'd been right.

At the moment, he was standing on the other side of the room, cradling his daughter and talking with his friends who'd come to visit from California. Their triplets, who were adorable, were toddling around with Hope's twins. The rest of her friends and family were clustered together in the house she now shared with Erik.

They'd decided to wait to get married until after Lily Grace was born. Or, rather, she'd refused until then. She'd dreamed of her wedding day for most of her life, and wanted to wait until she could focus on creating the perfect day for her and Erik.

Because she was sentimental, they'd decided to get married over Memorial Day weekend, one year from the day Erik had barreled back into her life. Plenty of time for her to fit into the amazing wedding dress Willow was designing for her.

Happiness settled bone-deep as she surveyed the family around her.

Colt rolled up next to her. "You look happy."

"I am," she said, unable to suppress a wide grin.

"You should be. She's amazing, Lo. You did good."

Lola sighed. "Yeah."

Scooting a little closer, Colt bumped her gently with the edge of his wheel, trying to get her undivided attention. Looking down at him, she raised a single eyebrow.

"I know this isn't the best time to say this, but with everything happening the last few weeks, there just hasn't been another opportunity."

"What's up, Colt?"

"I'm leaving Bliss Photography."

Lola laughed, bending a little closer so she could hear her brother better. "It sounded like you just said you're leaving Bliss."

"I am. I've loved working for you over the last few years. You have no idea how much I needed the work or the outlet, especially in the beginning."

Oh, she did. That was why she'd given him the job in the first place. When Colt had first been released after his accident, adjustment had not come easy. He'd needed purpose and she'd been determined to give him one.

But he'd quickly become damn good at his job. He handled the details that she was too distracted to pay attention to. There was no way Bliss would be as successful without him running the show behind the scenes.

"You can't leave. What am I going to do without you?"

Colt smiled. "You'll be fine. I've been interviewing replacements for the last two weeks."

"You've been what?" How the hell had she missed this?

"You've been a little preoccupied. And I didn't want to add anything else to your plate. But I don't have another choice. I start my new position in a week. I've hired a wonderful woman who's new to Sweetheart. She'd got experience and the backbone to put up with your mouth, and I'm pretty sure she needs this job more than I ever did."

Well, that sounded like a story she'd want to get later, but right now she was still stuck on *new position*.

"I thought we agreed that you'd tell me when you started looking for a job in your field, Colt. I always knew you'd want to do something with your degree when you finished it."

Her brother would graduate just days before her wedding…

"I know, and that's what I'd planned to do. But an opportunity that I couldn't pass up fell into my lap. I'm going to be working with a clinic in Charleston, helping others deal with the emotional trauma of accidents like mine. Police officers, firefighters, soldiers, children… Lo, I couldn't say no."

"Of course not." She wouldn't want him to. This was exactly what he'd spent the last several years working toward.

Colt snagged her arm and pulled her down until all of his strength was wrapped around her shoulders in a hug so fierce it could have righted the world. "I'm sorry for the timing, but you're going to be fine. You don't need me here anymore. You've got Erik."

Her brother let her go and immediately, Lola's gaze found Erik across the room. A gentle smile tugged at her lips. "Yeah."

Erik looked up, catching her eye. The burst of joy she saw there had her own heart clenching in answer. They'd had their moments over the last few months, but they were learning to deal with issues together. She watched as he nuzzled their daughter's head, filling his lungs with what he called the baby smell.

Lola laughed, shaking her head.

Her dad swooped in and coaxed Lily Grace out of Erik's arms. For the first few days she'd been out of the hospital, Lola had refereed more than a few fights over who got to hold her daughter between those two. But they'd since come to an understanding.

Weaving through their friends, Erik slipped up behind her, wrapping his arms around her waist and pulling her close.

"Did you know Colt took a job in Charleston and is

leaving Bliss?" she asked, craning her neck around to spear him with a look.

"Put the glare away, Lo. I just found out yesterday, but he asked me not to say anything until he had a chance to talk to you."

Lola harrumphed but leaned back against him anyway. "He's even hired his replacement."

"Of course he has."

"Maybe I wanted some input."

"So let the woman go if you don't mesh well."

Leaning down, Erik found the spot right beneath her ear that always had her entire body tingling, and sucked.

"That kind of distraction isn't going to work. I'm irritated."

"Yeah, but for once it's not all at me. And don't think I've forgotten the doctor cleared you for all *activity* today at your appointment. Six weeks is a damn long time, Lola."

His mouth roamed, suffusing her with light and heat, making her dizzy in the most delicious way. No matter what else was between them, Erik always knew exactly how to send her body up in flames.

"I need to get my hands on you," he growled.

"We have a house full of people, Erik." But God, she wanted the same thing.

"Later," she promised.

"Later and for always."

* * * * *

COMING NEXT MONTH FROM

HARLEQUIN® *Blaze*®

Available May 23, 2017

#943 ONE NIGHT WITH A SEAL (anthology)
Uniformly Hot!
by Tawny Weber and Beth Andrews
What could be sexier than twin Navy SEAL brothers searching for their happily-ever-afters? Read the ultimate Uniformly Hot! Blaze—two stories in one!

#944 OFF LIMITS MARINE
by Kate Hoffmann
After her husband died, Annie Foster Jennings swore she'd never marry another military man. But if anyone can change her mind, it's sweet, sexy pilot Gabe Pendleton.

#945 EASY RIDE
by Suzanne Ruby
Aspiring reporter Kirby Montgomery goes undercover at an exclusive club. But when she falls for the subject of her story, Adam Drake—nickname Easy Ride—all bets are off.

#946 NOTORIOUS
by Vicki Lewis Thompson
When rancher Noah Garfield spots Keely Branscom in Sin City, he decides it's his duty to reform the bad girl from his past. Which should be easy...unless Keely tempts him with her wild ways!

*One SEAL can be trouble...but when two sexy SEAL twin
brothers return home on leave for a high school reunion,
anything can happen!*

*Read on for a sneak preview of
ONE NIGHT WITH A SEAL.
Enjoy two linked novellas in one book—
"All Out" by* New York Times *bestselling author
Tawny Weber
&
"All In" by* RITA® *Award–winning author
Beth Andrews.*

"The Bennett brothers are coming home?"

A thrill of delight shot through Vivian Harris at the
news.

"Yep, Xander and Zane should be here—" Mike
looked at his watch and grinned "—within the hour."

"Both of them?" At her brother's scowl, Vivian made
a show of sweeping her long blond bangs away from her
face and giving him a wide-eyed look of concern. "Are
you sure Little Creek can handle an invasion by the Bad
Boy Bennetts?"

"Probably not," Mike replied with a laugh. "Luckily
they're only here for ten days. Other than breaking a few
hearts, I don't think they can do much damage with so
little time."

"Last time they were only home a week and they got
into a huge bar fight after you challenged them to see

who could drink the most shots. They broke the table at the diner arm wrestling, and if rumor is correct, they were seen streaking down Main Street at three in the morning as part of some insane decathlon." Oh, how she'd wept over missing that sight.

"Nah, the streaking was just a rumor. But the rest are true." Mike's grin widened. "I'm going to have to do some serious thinking if I'm going to top all of those challenges."

Vivian had a few challenges she wouldn't mind offering Zane. Talk about a dream worth living—if only for ten days.

Her fingers tapping a beat on the scarred surface of the bakery counter, Vivian gave herself a minute to delve into her favorite fantasy. The one that starred her and Zane Bennett covered in nothing but chocolate frosting and a few tempting dollops of whipped cream.

Maybe it was time to try out a few of her dreams on something other than her bakery business. After all, if she could make a glistening penis-shaped cake worthy of oohs and ahhs, how hard could it be to get her hands on Zane Bennett's real one?

Vivian flashed a wicked smile.

Hopefully, once she got her hands on it, it'd be very, very hard.

Don't miss
ONE NIGHT WITH A SEAL
by Tawny Weber and Beth Andrews.

Available June 2017 wherever
Harlequin Blaze books and ebooks are sold.

www.Harlequin.com